BATTLE FLEET

Also by Paul Dowswell

Powder Monkey
Prison Ship

Adventures of a Young Sailor

BATTLE FLEET

Paul Dowswell

BLOOMSBURY

First published in Great Britain in 2007 by Bloomsbury Publishing Plc
Published in the United States in 2008 by Bloomsbury U.S.A. Children's Books
175 Fifth Avenue, New York, New York 10010
Distributed to the trade by Macmillan

Library of Congress Cataloging-in-Publication Data
available upon request
ISBN-13: 978-1-59990-080-3 • ISBN-10: 1-59990-080-7

First U.S. Edition 2008
Typeset by Dorchester Typesetting Group Ltd
Printed in the U.S.A. by Quebecor World Fairfield
1 3 5 7 9 10 8 6 4 2

To
DD
and
J & J

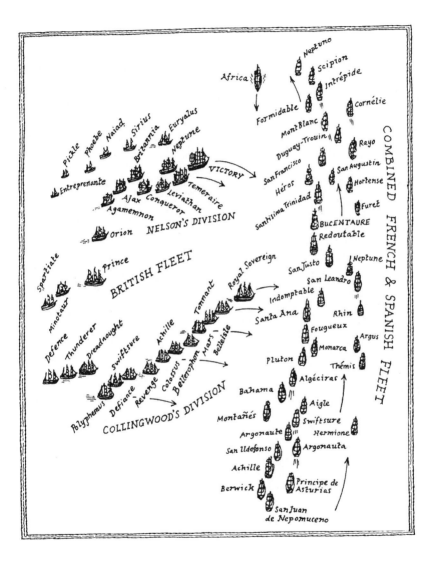

21st October 1805,
shortly before noon

Contents

This is a dream that will not leave me. I am propped against the quarterdeck rail on a stricken man-o'-war. I have been wounded and cannot move. Although it is daytime, all around is darkness – from a murky sky and smoke that pours from a fo'c'sle fire. Despite the heat of the blaze and the warm, cloying breeze blowing across the ship, I feel cold sweat running down my back. No one else is there. I am alone on the deck but can hear anguished cries from below. I close my eyes, consumed by dread, and wish with all my heart I had never gone to sea . . .

Chapter 1

Goodbye to All That

We sailed from Sydney on a perfect spring day, out into the blustery winds of the Pacific Ocean. Richard stood beside me atop the foremast with a huge grin on his face. 'This is a voyage I never thought we'd make again,' he said. 'Certainly not as free men.'

I looked down on our ship the *Orion*, and thought what a handsome vessel she was. Three masts to speed us through the oceans, twenty-four guns to protect us. Despite these guns there was still no mistaking her for a man-o'-war. She had the plump curves of a merchant vessel, and would make a tempting prize for any pirate or privateer who crossed our path. The crew would never pass muster on a Royal Navy ship either.

The *Orion* had visited Sydney to sell – plates, buckles, shoes – rather than buy. She had taken on a small quantity of timber and flax, and us. The crew had also loaded a large number of botanical specimens, each in their own separately marked pot, to be shipped back to England. Then they had stocked up on fresh water, fruit and fowl for the journey. Where there was space beside the plants, the weather deck was packed with caged birds, their constant squawking adding to the general pandemonium.

A haughty Scottish voice called up from below. 'Look lively, you urchins on the fore topgallant!' That could only be Lieutenant Hossack, the ship's second in command. We had been on the *Orion* for less than a day, and already I had taken a strong dislike to him.

When we came down to the deck, he was waiting and gave me a swift clout around the ear. 'I'll not tolerate slackers, Witchall,' he said. 'You'll pull your weight on this voyage, or you'll find yourself with some stripes on your back.'

When my duties were over, I went to sit on the fo'c'sle, alone with my thoughts. Evening fell, a beautiful velvety evening, like a warm, starry blanket. A cool breeze cut through the heat and I filled my lungs to bursting, feeling light-headed with happiness. For the first time in perhaps six months I was free from a crushing, ever-present fear of death.

Richard came to join me. We had sailed together since I was first pressed aboard HMS *Miranda* three years before. After fighting side by side at Copenhagen we had been framed by our ship's crooked Purser. Transported together as convicts to New South Wales we had now been pardoned and freed to return home.

He had joined the Royal Navy as his family in Massachusetts believed it would be the best apprentice-ship for a boy with the sea in his bones. Now he had had enough. When we reached the East Indies port of Coupang, he planned to hook up with an American ship and work his passage home to Boston.

I was pleased to sit with him, of course, but I felt a twinge of betrayal over his plans to leave. We ought to look after each other. Especially on this ship. They were a rough bunch, the crew, and worse than the merchant seamen I'd known when I first went to sea.

We got some measure of them that afternoon, when there was a tussle on the fo'c'sle. Two seamen started arguing about a harbour girl who had tried to solicit their favour and they began to fight. Several of their fellows gathered around. Rather than pulling them apart, they started throwing stones and other missiles at them.

The Captain, Henry Evison, waded in, banged their heads together and had them both clapped in irons.

'I expect the press gangs have taken the best merchant seamen,' said Richard. 'Half of this lot don't even know their way around the rigging. The other half seem pretty good, though I'd hate to see them with some drink inside them.'

Along with half a dozen passengers, there were only thirty or so men in the crew. They were a curious collection of old salts, chancers, rogues and shirkers. There were colliermen from Newcastle trying their hand at deep-water sailing, a few former slavers, and rogues from the postal packets who boasted openly of their smuggling rackets. Toughest of the lot were the gruff northerners known as Greenlandmen – those who had made long voyages into the Arctic, hunting for humpback and right whales.

They were a breed apart and on that first evening I enjoyed listening to their boastful tales while we ate, especially the stories about escaping the press gang. They were not above a bloody battle when the Navy tried to board their whalers, and would drive them off with harpoon and grapeshot. One of the Greenlandmen, William Bedlington, was a bearded giant – six foot three – as he told us several times.

'So how did you end up at sea?' he asked me.

I told him I'd joined a merchantman at Great Yarmouth and been caught by a Navy press gang.

'I got pressed the once,' he said. 'Came and took me from me bunk they did, night before we sailed out of Hull. Before I knew it I were plonked in a boat with a bayonet at me belly and they were rowing for the quay. Soon sorted that lot out. I pressed against the strakes with me back and me feet and broke that boat in half before they realised what I were doin'. Bastards all drowned – that'll teach 'em not to learn to swim.'

It sounded an unlikely tale. Later that night I heard Bedlington claim to have jumped a five-bar gate with his wife under one arm. I wondered if they were still together.

Rough men I could cope with, there were plenty like them in the Navy after all. I hated our cramped quarters though. The crew were packed into a couple of filthy cabins in the fo'c'sle and the stink in there was unbearable. Part of the smell came from the fetid bedding – there were bunks here rather than hammocks I was used to at sea. Evison was keen to keep the rest of his ship spick and span they told me, but he turned a blind eye to the seamen's quarters. It was so stuffy the candles would not burn for want of air.

Early next day we suggested a good clean up of our cabin, but we got short shrift. 'There's enough bloody scrubbing of the decks to do,' said Bedlington, 'wi'out havin' to do ower own quarters. I like a bit o' dirt meself. Keeps the flux and pox at bay.'

The *Orion* was a creaking, leaky old vessel and Richard and I were quickly put to work caulking the decks and strakes. The ship was rumoured to be stricken with teredo worm too. On a quiet night, it was said, you could hear the dull scratching sound of them gnawing away at the timbers of the hull. I knew there were stormy seas ahead and I hoped the *Orion* would be strong enough to survive them.

Despite our year away, Richard and I still had that Navy sense of discipline and duty – an instinct to do a job properly, for the good of the ship and its crew. When we tended to repairs, we would do it until the job was done. This annoyed the other men working alongside us who tried to do as little as they could get away with. When I tried to show one of the crew how to do a monkey's fist knot on a rope he was using, I heard oaths that even convicts on a transport ship would shrink from using.

After those first few days Richard and I began to feel increasingly uncomfortable with the crew. They would barely talk to us when we ate our meals, and we would be jostled on the decks or companionways as men walked past. Occasionally one would spit on the deck close to where we were scrubbing it. 'Maybe they're like this with all new sailors?' I said.

Richard shrugged. 'Never mind. We've got each other for company.'

We didn't like the crew but we did like Evison. He was a tall, gruff Lancastrian who spoke with his fists if any man showed disrespect or acted foolishly. But he fed his crew the best he could and treated them fairly. I sensed we were in safe hands.

'I think the Captain's all right,' said Richard. 'Bit of a rough diamond though. Have you heard the stories about him? Spent his whole life at sea. They say he knows neither his exact age or his real name. He was found as a small boy, drifting off the coast of South America, the only survivor in a boat of castaways. Wouldn't like to get on the wrong side of him though.'

I laughed. 'Never mind him, it's his wife I'm frightened of.'

'Not as much as he is,' said Richard.

Evison's wife Kitty was a great stout woman, plain in her likes and dislikes. Like him she was also from Lancashire. When we had been brought to the *Orion*, she had been against our joining the crew. 'They're boys, Mr Evison,' she had said to our faces, after we had been added to the muster book. 'You want strapping tars who can do everything they're called on to do, not these. Let 'em travel as passengers, if they've got the means to pay.'

'They're Navy lads, Mrs Evison,' said the Captain patiently. 'I'm sure they'll do us proud. And I'll wager they can do more than most of the other sailors on this ship.'

'Make sure you do, boys,' she said, fixing us with a flinty eye.

Among the other women on board was Lizzie Borrow, the daughter of one of the Governor's officials. She was fleeing back to England after a disastrous engagement to an army officer. This was good news for Richard, who had taken a fancy to her. Lizzie had a maid too – a pretty dark-haired girl called Bel Sparke. Lizzie was occasionally friendly, although she could be haughty too. I had never spoken to Bel, but I felt drawn to her. She had an impish smile and I longed to know more about her.

As we sailed further north, the lush shore began to turn a sickly green as the climate grew hotter and drier. We were making a cracking pace through the breakers and warm wind.

I was surprised how quickly I adapted to life at sea after our year in New South Wales. The food was no worse than what we'd have expected on a Navy ship – the usual salt meat, pease and biscuit – though there was a particularly revolting barrel of salt pork filled with feet and tails still covered with hair, and even the head of a pig with a ring running through its nose.

Our day was little different from that of a Navy ship. Two watches for the crew, four hours on four hours off. Inspection every Saturday and then the crew exercised with the guns and practised their small arms drill. It was a relief to see they were pretty handy with the weapons.

'D'you know much about where we're going?' said Richard over dinner.

'The Spice Islands? They sound exciting,' I said. On the voyage out here, we had sailed straight from the Cape to the south coast of New South Wales. Now we were heading north to the great ring of islands above the continent, and would then bear west to Africa.

'They're excitin' all right,' said John Garrick, the bespectacled ship's carpenter, who was sitting opposite us. 'Excitin' like being chased by a pack of dogs is excitin',' he said in his West Country burr. 'If you don't catch some fatal disease when we pass through, then the pirates will get you . . . not a pretty story. The pirates in these waters come out forty boats at a time and kills every last man, woman and child on a European ship. And you've always got the chance of being killed by an earthquake or volcano.'

I thought they'd be a spectacular sight to witness and said, 'We'll be all right if we stick to our ship.'

'Sailed these waters before have you?' said Garrick

sharply. 'Thought not. Your earthquakes are followed by giant tidal waves that sweep a ship away in an instant. The natives call them tsunamis.'

'No matter,' I told myself. What could be more dangerous than going into battle? We'd done that. We were tough enough to take anything the sea could throw at us.

We talked more about the port of Coupang, on Timor Island, where Richard hoped to find an American ship. Garrick was full of gloomy advice here too. 'You'd be better off at Batavia – that's the main trading port around here. You'd have more ships to pick from. But we're not going there, which is a good thing for the rest of us. It's full of Dutch and they say a thousand of 'em die a year from disease.'

Garrick really didn't like the East Indies, and there was no stopping him. He was making me feel uneasy and I wished he'd shut up.

'I can't be doin' with the natives round here, either. "They're ugly and strong, and bear malice long" – that's what the Dutch say about 'em. Much rather be doin' business with the Indian or Chinaman. But the Captain don't want to go that way. They say he hasn't got a proper licence – and if the East India Company catch him there'll be trouble.'

I didn't know what he was talking about, and I certainly didn't like the sound of it. He could see the baffled look on our faces.

'East India Company – they've got the sole right to trade for Britain east of the Cape. You go further than Cape Town you gotta be an East Indiaman. Evison thinks he can beat 'em by trading with New South Wales and the Spice Islands. "Who'll know?" he says. Maybe he's right. There's very little British trade in these islands, so maybe we'll get away with it.'

'What sort of highwayman outfit is this?' said Richard sharply. 'No licence to trade! What will happen if we get caught? Will we get treated like pirates?'

'Don't soil yerself over that, lad,' said Garrick impatiently. 'Evison'll be fined, that's all. Anyway. I'll not have you talkin' about the Captain like that. He's a good man, and he knows what he's doin'.'

I felt a bit bashful about the way Garrick spoke to us. He was a decent sort, and a seasoned tar, but like many of the crew he seemed to have taken a dislike to us. Maybe we were being a bit too cocky?

I was also shaken up by the other things he'd said. A leaky ship without a licence to trade. A pirate-infested sea. A pestilence-ridden land. The chill of impending disaster crept into my bones.

CHAPTER 2

Bird Trouble

'Put your back into it, Witchall,' said Lieutenant Hossack, as we scrubbed the deck one morning. 'I'll not tolerate slackers.'

'Yes, sir, right away, sir, at once, sir . . .' I tugged my forelock in mock respect. But just as I caught myself wondering if I had gone too far, I noticed Hossack had wandered off. He had not even noticed I was poking fun at him.

'Ai'll nut tolerayt slackahs, Witchull,' said Richard, imitating the Lieutenant's demure Edinburgh accent. 'Us, slackers?' he said. 'We work harder than anyone else on this leaky bucket. Watch him though, he can still have you flogged.'

Hossack's bullying was shared equally among the crew. And his pious righteousness. He would suffer no swearing: 'The Lord abhors an uncouth man,' I heard him say as he rained down blows on Thomas Bagley, one of the Newcastle colliers he had overheard let slip a curse. Bagley was a big man, fond of his pie and ale, so at least the Lieutenant didn't just victimise us boys.

Captain Evison caught my eye and beckoned me over. I thought he was going to admonish me too, but instead he said, 'Witchall – are you good with animals?'

'I looked after the ship's cat on HMS *Miranda*, sir. And I grew up in the country.'

'That'll do,' he said, then beckoned me to follow him into his cabin.

The interior was quite different from that of a Navy captain's quarters. There was no sparkling silver and burnished wood, just dull furnishings among a lot of clutter and a large table with a map spread upon it. The cabin was in need of a lick of paint. But on the balcony outside the stern windows there was an explosion of colour. Evison had rows of potted plants – lemons, oranges and limes, all sprouting and fruiting.

Something squawked in the corner. It was a large bird, perhaps two whole foot from beak to tail, and white all over, aside from a tuft of yellow feathers on its head.

Some of its other feathers lay ruffled on its body. The bird caught my eye and began flapping around as far as its short tether would allow.

'Show us yer arse,' it said by way of greeting.

Evison sighed. 'I'm afraid the Governor left it in the care of a squad of marines.' There was a pause where he raised his eyes to heaven. 'He's asked me to deliver it to his friend Lord Montague in London. Mrs Evison has had enough of it already and I haven't the time to look after it. The thing needs a lot of attention. Will you take care of it?'

'I'll try, sir, but I've never looked after a parrot before. I imagine he's a bit lonely. I've seen them in the wild, and they always flock together with their kind.'

'It's a cockatoo, I'm told, not a parrot. A sulphur crested cockatoo, no less. Thing's wasting away. I've tried feeding it biscuit, rats, mice, bacon, cheese, and the creature just nibbles a bit then turns up its beak. I'm sure it were bigger when it came on board.'

I had seen similar creatures out in the bush, and I could take a good guess at what it would eat. 'Perhaps we could give it fruit, sir?'

Evison looked affronted. 'Feed this thing the antiscorbutics we've got on board and the crew would mutiny. Keeping my men's scurvy at bay is more important than keeping this creature alive.'

'But what about the botanical samples on deck?' I

said. 'Can't we take fruit from them when they produce it?' Half the ship's waist was covered in potted plants, each clearly marked 'To the Royal Botanical Gardens, Kew'. 'Does it have a name, sir, do you know?'

'Mrs Evison calls it "that ruddy bird", but I don't think that's helping encourage it to make more elevated conversation. You give it a name, Witchall, and try and teach it to say something else.'

'I think we should call him Sydney, sir.'

'Sydney it is. And let's assume it's a he. I'm blowed if I know.'

We went to the waist to inspect the plants. There were bushes bearing raspberry-like fruit. I plucked two or three berries, and when I offered them to Sydney back at the Captain's quarters he almost bit my hand off.

I took him to my quarters, which I shared with ten other seamen. They hated the bird at first sight, and began to torment him – squawking and strutting in bird-like motions around his perch. This is another way of getting at me, I thought. During the next week I tried to teach Sydney some new words, but while my back was turned my companions were hard at work too. I came in one day and Sydney said 'Please kill me' over and over. At least none of them had actually been mean enough to do it yet.

To match his cheery greeting, he was a miserable bird and his beak seemed to be causing him distress – it looked like the top and bottom were growing into each other. Sydney often tried to bite his perch, but it was difficult for him to do. I went to see Garrick, the carpenter, and he gave me a few strips of rotting wood. He was nicer to me this time.

'I can see you're both good lads and good sailors too,' he said as he rooted round his little workshop. 'This crew, they're not the finest bunch, but they're shapin' up. Best not to look down on 'em too much. It's a long voyage to spend with men you don't rub along with.' I wasn't going to defend myself. I knew he was right.

'That bird's not makin' you very popular neither,' he said. 'But you stick it out. They'll get to like him. There's months of this ahead and every one needs somethin' to entertain 'em.'

Sydney grabbed a sliver of wood at once in one claw and, balancing on the other foot, immediately began to gnaw away. From then on, Garrick made a point of giving him a bit of wood to chew whenever he could spare one. I supposed that Sydney's beak grew like our fingernails do. If he'd nothing to gnaw on, it would curve inward and kill him.

He could be an affectionate bird when you got to know him. He especially liked me to stroke his neck and his back, and would even lower his head when I came near him if he wanted me to pet him. He was quite open in his feelings though. For those who teased him he had a peck and a squawk, although this seemed to encourage them.

I thought he would enjoy being out in the open so I persuaded Evison to let me take him on deck for a few hours a day. 'He'll like being with the other birds,' I said.

But out in the fresh air, Sydney took no interest in the caged birds. Instead he would stare longingly at the seabirds that circled our ship and try to fly away from his perch. I did feel sorry for him. I knew what it was like to be held captive.

Looking after Sydney might make me more unpopular with the crew but it had one great perk. It gave me and Richard an excuse to talk to Lizzie and Bel. Like the other passengers, who often took to wandering the weather deck in a sullen daze, they were finding the voyage very tedious. Sydney was the perfect distraction. When I took him out on deck, they often came over to see him.

'Lucky you,' Lizzie said to me, 'having this lovely creature to look after. I'm sure it passes the time most pleasurably.' She sounded rather wistful and turned to Bel. 'Think of all the things we could teach him to say! I wonder what other tricks he could do?' Then she turned back to me. 'Don't you find it a trial though, having to take care of Sydney as well as perform all your other duties on the ship?'

I could see where she was going here, and I wanted to keep Sydney for myself. Bel caught my eye and said, 'They make a terrible mess, Miss Lizzie. Might be too much trouble. Besides, Sam here is doing such a good job. You can tell Sydney likes him.'

Lizzie and Bel were a pair of opposites. Lizzie was tall and buxom, with blonde curly hair and peachy skin. Bel was much smaller and had big grey eyes in a face pale against a thick black mane of hair. Although they were mistress and servant, they seemed more like close friends, but while Lizzie spoke with the measured tone and poise of the wealthy heiress she was, Bel was a cockney girl.

Richard came over to join us. Lizzie gave him a dazzling smile. 'It's our American friend. Are you a bird lover too?'

'Never had one of these myself, Miss Lizzie,' he said, 'but he's a handsome creature.'

'I prefer to be addressed as Miss Borrow,' said Lizzie rather frostily. I wasn't sure whether she was teasing or being serious.

Richard sailed blithely on. 'So, how are you finding the voyage?'

'Very dull,' she said. 'And so much more tedious on a merchant ship than one of the transports.'

'Really!' said Richard in genuine surprise. We had

sailed over with Lizzie the previous year, when we had been transported. 'Oh yes,' she said archly. 'With a ship full of you rough convict types there was always the chance there'd be a mutiny and we'd have our throats slit. That was far more exciting. The only thing we'll die of here is boredom.'

Then they sauntered off to the fo'c'sle. Bel looked around to catch my eye. I wasn't sure whether she was saying 'Well that told you!' or 'Don't mind her.'

Richard was not discouraged by Lizzie's haughtiness. 'Plenty of time to get to know the girls,' he said after they'd gone. 'Only so much you can do on a ship – they'll be eager for the company of a couple of handsome lads like us!' I envied his confidence, and wondered where he'd got it. As far as I knew, Richard had never kissed a girl in his life.

Unsurprisingly, Richard wasn't the only young man on the *Orion* who fancied his chances with Lizzie Borrow. When he and I were both high in the rigging shortening one of the mizzen topsails, the sound of Lizzie's laughter floated up to us. Hossack had invited her to join him on the quarterdeck during his watch. 'Don't fall for him,' said Richard between gritted teeth. 'He's pompous. He walks around like he's got a poker stuck up his backside and I'll bet he sips his tea with his little finger cocked up in the air.' The two of them were deep in conversation. 'Walk away,' said Richard. 'Come and talk to me instead when I get down from this mast. I'm more interesting. And I'm not a bully! And I'm much better looking!'

Richard was at a disadvantage when it came to wooing a wealthy girl like Lizzie Borrow. Not least because Hossack could invite Lizzie to the officer's cabin, where they could dine on fine food and wine from a lace tablecloth. Bel would accompany her, of course, as a chaperone. I wondered if Hossack had asked them yet. I felt a twinge of jealousy. 'Never mind,' I said. 'We'll be officers one day. Then we'll be irresistible!'

'Witchall and Buckley,' Hossack's voice called up from below. 'Attend to your duties, and stop gossiping like a couple of giddy lassies.'

'Now he's just showing off,' I said, but Richard flushed angrily.

The crew continued to give me a hard time about my cockatoo. William Bedlington picked me up by my shirt one morning and lifted me so close to his face I could smell his stinking breath and see the crumbs of food in his beard. 'Have that thing fed some rat poison, something to kill it without Evison suspecting. I've had enough of it, and so has every other damn man in this cabin.'

They had good cause to complain – when you had only four hours to sleep you did not want to be disturbed by a flapping, squawking bird. Fortunately the crew's complaints reached Evison's ears too, and he acted swiftly. 'Witchall,' he told me, 'you are going to have your own cabin – a small one, by the other passengers. You'll have to share it with Sydney. But well done, lad, the bird's starting to look a lot better these days.'

'Won't the passengers mind, sir? He can be very noisy!'

'Damn the passengers. If they mutiny, they'll be easily dealt with. Can't say that for the crew.'

I couldn't believe my luck. A cabin of my own. Richard was green with envy.

The cabin was small, with a tiny porthole of dingy green glass to let in a little light. There was no room for a bunk and barely enough room to swing the hammock I was given. But I still felt very privileged. I placed Sydney's perch by the door, facing the porthole so he could see something of the outside world. It was the first time I had had a room of my own since I left home. It was a curious sensation being alone on a ship. On drowsy afternoons between watches I would lie there on my own, daydreaming about Bel.

Being out on deck suited Sydney, and he soon picked up a fine collection of nautical sayings, like 'Hoist the mizzen royal', 'Tighten the shrouds' and 'Look lively, yer lubberly bastards'. He was a clever bird. He rarely said 'Show us yer arse' any more, except to Mrs Evison.

Two weeks after we left the northern coast Richard came screaming down below deck with distressing news. 'Sydney's slipped his mooring.'

I ran up to the perch where I'd left him on deck. His tether dangled down, severed close to the knot.

Mrs Evison walked past as we stood there inspecting the scene of the crime. 'Pecked his way to freedom has he?' she smirked. 'Can't say I'll miss him much.'

'I'll bet it was you,' I thought.

I did feel miserable. Poor old Sydney lost at sea. What a fate. But then I stopped feeling sorry for the bird and started to worry about losing my cabin. Evison wouldn't let me keep it if I didn't have a cockatoo to look after. I would be back in the fo'c'sle with the rest of the crew. And we'd have less of an excuse to talk to the girls. Maybe it wasn't Mrs Evison who'd cut the tether after all. Maybe one of the crew had done it out of spite.

Three hours later, Garrick spotted Sydney circling the ship from a distance. Had he escaped while the coast was still in sight I'm sure he would have been gone for good. Perhaps he realised he was lost and we were his only source of food and company. Dragging his tether behind him must have tired him out.

We shouted ourselves hoarse. 'Sydney! Come back!' Lizzie and Bel came out to wave their hats.

He landed on the main topsail and there he stayed,

right at the end of the yardarm.

Everyone seemed pleased to see him, except Mrs Evison. 'Clear off y'bloody bird,' she shouted.

The following morning he was still up there. We held up berries and nuts, but nothing could shift him from his perch. 'Perhaps he thinks you're angry with him, Sam,' said Bel. 'D'you think you ought to go and get him?'

Armed with a slice of apple I shinned up the shrouds and tried to coax him down. I expected him to be pleased to see me, but he wasn't. As I balanced on the rope beneath the yard, the wretched bird flew right at my face. My feet slipped and I dropped the apple. I clung on for dear life to the top of the yard with my feet scrabbling for the rope, and then Sydney started to peck at my hand.

'The bird's gone mad. Get a musket and shoot it,' squawked Mrs Evison.

'Sydney, stop it!' I yelled, and he backed off. I found my footing and came down again to the deck. I was trembling now and could see the girls had both gone white with anxiety.

Bel ran up to me. 'Sam, we thought you were goin' to fall.'

Perhaps it was foolish of me to risk my life to help that bird. Maybe it was to impress the girls, or keep the cabin, even to spite Mrs Evison. Maybe it was because I had grown fond of him too. I found that slice of apple on the deck and went straight back up the rigging. This time Sydney came quietly. First he bowed his head to let me stroke him. Then he picked up the apple, carefully nibbling away the flesh from the skin with his beak. Then he hopped on my shoulder and I skimmed down the ratlines to the deck.

The girls came to make a fuss of him. I was the hero of the hour. Bel was convinced Sydney was a girl. 'Maybe she's gone all broody,' she cooed in a way that made me lose sleep for a week. 'She's probably missing her mate.'

By now the crew had noticed how well we got on with the girls, and it became something else for them to taunt us with. 'It's the budding Casanovas,' said William Bedlington whenever he saw us on the fo'c'sle. 'Give the girls a kiss from me,' he'd leer. It wasn't outright bullying, but like the little digs when we were holystoning the deck, or the shoves on the companionways, it was their way of telling us they didn't like us.

CHAPTER 3

A Whiff of Sulphur

First we saw thin columns of smoke reaching up to the distant horizon, then mountain peaks, fuzzy through the heat haze, clearer as we grew nearer. Despite the danger we'd been told about, catching sight of the islands of the East Indies after the monotony of several weeks away from land was still exciting. We were making progress. 'I don't care how perilous they are, I'm volunteering for the first trip ashore,' I said to Richard. 'It'll be good to get away from this scurvy lot.'

The closer we got to land, the more it rained. We were

arriving in the middle of the wet season, where a sudden downpour would soak the dry timbers of the ship and bring a welcome cool to the heat of the day. But some days, as we sailed along that island chain, it would rain incessantly, and then everything and everyone would become drenched and soggy. Feeling cold was a novelty. After my time on the *Elephant* sailing through the North Sea at the tail end of winter, I never wanted to be that cold again.

Sighting land also meant we were another stage nearer to Coupang and the moment Richard would leave the ship was closer to hand. It wasn't just the fact that I'd miss him that troubled me. Maybe the crew would be nastier to me when he was no longer around. Maybe I'd see less of Bel too, as Lizzie would no longer be drawn over to talk to Richard.

We had shared a lot of our free time talking with the girls recently. Lizzie Borrow would never mingle with our kind in her normal life, but she was intrigued by Richard. She often asked him about life in the New World. He was not remotely bashful about her station in life compared to his. Although he was an ordinary seaman on this ship, I suppose his family had money, like hers, and he had prospects.

I sometimes wondered if this friendship would make Lieutenant Hossack jealous and he would take it out on Richard. But he was so sure of his own social superiority it didn't even occur to him that he might have a rival for Lizzie's affections.

The smoke we could see came from smouldering volcanoes on some of the islands. When we sailed into the wind, the air filled with the whiff of sulphur. I had hoped to see them spew rocks and fire into the sky, until Garrick told me that it would probably be the last thing I would see.

The older hands told us that terrifying creatures like tigers and black panthers lurked within the dense, emerald forests around these blunted peaks. I had seen such creatures in my father's books. There were dragons too – scaly monsters with forked tongues. And strange, hairy, orange creatures called orang-utans that were almost human. I strained my eyes at the shore, sometimes borrowing a telescope, but saw only the odd flash of colour as a parrot or cockatoo darted between the highest branches.

Sydney seemed indifferent to the far-off calls of his feathery kind. Perhaps he'd got used to life aboard the *Orion*, and liked the fuss we made of him and the food he was given three times a day.

Lizzie and Bel were frequently seen on deck, gazing excitedly towards the islands. 'We must ask the Captain to take us ashore,' I heard Lizzie say to Bel. 'What a treat for us to be away from the ship and to walk along one of those lovely beaches.' She turned to me. 'D'you think he'll let us? I get so restless on the ship. One does long for a change of scenery.'

'No harm in asking, Miss Lizzie,' I said. 'Maybe if Richard and me promise to look after you.'

She gave me one of her arch smiles and said nothing. I suspected she thought Lieutenant Hossack would be a more appropriate escort.

As we sailed past our first island, Evison called the crew together. 'Those of you unfamiliar with these waters take heed. Those who've been here before, let this act as a reminder. They can be treacherous, the Malays, and until we clear the northern shores of Sumatra I want the guns loaded and ready with round and grapeshot. We shall need a chest of arms upon the deck and the Bosun will see to it that there is always a lighted match to hand. The fo'c'sle, poop and gangways shall be constantly guarded. At night the officer of the watch will go round the ship once every quarter hour. And from eight o'clock at night the guards will call out 'All's well' at the same interval until the break of day. If we keep our wits about us, we will have a safe journey.'

I was surprised by his frankness. The passengers had not been summoned to hear the Captain's instructions but neither had any attempt been made to keep this information from them. Lizzie and Bel came out to listen and were clearly concerned. 'Teach us how to wield a pistol, Sam,' said Lizzie.

'Won't the Lieutenant show you?' I asked mischievously.

'The Lieutenant won't hear of it,' she said briskly.

Bel joined in. 'If we're attacked, I'm not goin' to have me throat slit without puttin' up a good fight, and neither's Lizzie.'

Evison forbade their use of firearms too when I asked him, but he did agree they should learn how to defend themselves. Out on the deck we ran through the moves we had learned aboard HMS *Miranda* – the strange, balletic steps of cutlass play that let the swordsman keep as great a distance as possible from his opponent. At first they were mocked by the crew. Lizzie was a bit lead-footed but Bel had a fluid grace about her and drew enough admiring glances to make me feel jealous.

One evening when I was talking to Bel on her own, she told me she was running out of books to read. 'Captain Evison has quite a collection in his cabin,' I said. 'Can you borrow some of his?'

'I'll have to get Lizzie to ask,' she said. 'He wouldn't lend them to me.'

'Who taught you to read?' I asked. I knew it was quite something for a poor London girl to be literate. She took my question as an excuse to tell me something about herself.

'Brought up in Bermondsey, I was,' she said. 'My ma's a fishwife at Billingsgate. My dad's a lighterman. We live and breathe by that River Thames. Neither of them can read a word. But I got taught by the vicar's missus. Wonderful lady she was. She took me off, told me how to make sense of them squiggles. My ma's ever so proud of me being able to read. My dad's not bothered though. "What bleedin' use is that?" he'd say. "You're a bleedin' girl!"

'I don't wanna spend the rest of my days guttin' fish like my ma. Not that she's thick or anything. She's sharp as a pin. But I want to see the world. That's why I'm happy to be with Miss Lizzie. She's a nice girl. Bit hoity-toity sometimes, still, no one's perfect. But she's taken me under her wing and taught me a lot.'

'Will you stay with her?' I asked.

'I'd be daft not to,' she said at once. 'She's my ticket out of the fish market. She's teaching me how to talk properly, good manners, the sort of things that stop people looking down their noses at you. I like the houses she lives in. I don't like the people she usually mingles with, but they're interesting. Most of them don't even look at me. I might as well be invisible. So I just melt into the background and watch.'

We both rested our arms on the starboard rail, staring

out to sea. She leaned a little closer. 'That Lieutenant, Hossack, he's taken quite a shine to her,' she whispered. 'I think she quite likes him too. She has a soft spot for gentlemen in uniform, unfortunately.'

I was pleased Bel liked me enough to confide in me. As she talked, I looked at the side of her face in the setting sun and thought how pretty she was. I wondered if one day I might dare to kiss her.

The *Orion* caught a sudden squall, and as the sails billowed, the hull lurched in the water. Bel and I slipped together awkwardly, just as she noticed me looking at her.

'Get yer saucy hands off me!' she said, shrugging me off with a giggle.

I meant to protest it was unintended, but thought that would make too much of the incident. Besides, Bel carried on talking as if nothing had happened. But she stayed out of my way for a few days after that, and I sank into a deep gloom. Richard kept asking me why I looked so glum. I didn't want to tell him. I felt guilty and I didn't know why. Had I revealed my feelings for Bel too obviously? Had she really thought I'd tried to embrace her? Perhaps we shouldn't even have been there, almost alone on deck at twilight?

Then one bright morning I saw three porpoises sporting just before the bow, weaving in and out of the water in an intricate dance. Bel was up on deck taking the air, and without thinking I called her over, before hurrying off on my duties. She stayed for a good while, laughing to herself, mesmerised by the sight.

Later that day, she came over when she saw me on the deck. 'Thanks, Sam, for showing me those big fish this morning. They were marvellous.' I had been forgiven.

By strange coincidence the Captain called Richard and I to his cabin the next morning. 'Mrs Evison here is worried that you boys might be up to something with the girls,' he said.

'Aye,' said Mrs Evison, who was sitting by the window. 'Especially Richard here and Miss Lizzie.'

Richard blushed deep crimson. 'My intentions towards Miss Borrow are honourable, Mrs Evison,' he spluttered.

She gave a dull chuckle. 'There's as much chance of that as getting drunk on brandy mince pies.'

Richard was affronted. 'I can assure you –'

She cut him off. 'You can talk with the girls as much as you like, there's precious little else to do on a long voyage. But if I catch even a whisper of a rumour of any carrying on, then your wedding tackle will be dangling from the mizzen yard.'

Richard was too stunned to reply.

Then she turned to me. 'Don't you go getting any ideas about Miss Sparke either.'

Now it was my turn to blush. I nearly said, 'Don't

worry, I won't be getting so much as a peck on the cheek from Miss Sparke', but I held my tongue.

'Once a girl is ruined she's as good as finished in society,' said Mrs Evison, trying to justify our scolding. 'And you'll never see a lady's maid with a baby. I like those two girls and I'm making it my business to look after them. So, think on, boys. Think on.'

We were dismissed. Back on deck we giggled like naughty schoolboys. 'Wedding tackle!' said Richard with a snigger. He'd never heard that one before.

I don't know whether the fear of pirate attack had made him uneasy but Lieutenant Hossack's behaviour grew more brutal and objectionable by the day. Every order that was not obeyed in an instant was met by violence. I noticed Captain Evison having a quiet word with him on the quarterdeck, and wondered if he was telling his Lieutenant to moderate his behaviour. Hossack had taken to waiting at the foot of a mast, whenever men had been sent to lengthen or shorten the sail, and hitting the last man down from the tops. It seemed only a matter of time before one of them would slip in his haste to return to the deck and plunge to his death. Hossack also made a habit of hitting the last man on deck when all hands were called.

One dark evening, when a storm was brewing, we were all ordered up and rushed from our bunks to shorten the sails. Hossack was there, by the forward companionway, waiting for the last man to come out to the weather deck. I rushed past him and into the blackest night I had seen for months. A new moon and cloudy sky meant you could barely see your hand in front of your face. Was I the last one? I expected him to hit me, but someone else was clattering up the companionway behind me.

Hossack punched the man who came after, telling him he was a 'tardy sluggard'. His victim immediately hit back with a punch that floored the Lieutenant. 'You'll be flogged for this,' Hossack shouted indignantly from the deck.

'I don't think so, Lieutenant,' said Captain Evison, for it was him Hossack had hit. 'In fact, I understand striking the Captain is a capital offence.'

Every man on deck heard this exchange. I supposed the two of them sorted out the matter between them, but from then on, the beating stopped, although Hossack would still bellow at us as if we were cattle on the way to market.

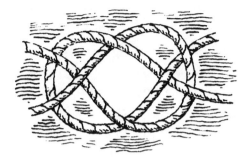

CHAPTER 4

'Run Out the Guns!'

Shortly after noon, a fortnight into our voyage through the islands, the lookout called, 'Ship off the starboard bow.' We ran over to the rail to see what was approaching. Sailing out from the bay of a nearby island was a fair-sized prau, as I had learned the natives called their sailing boats. There was only one, which was a relief, as Garrick had told us pirates often attacked in fleets of as many as fifty ships.

The vessel was making a line for us. 'Run out the guns,' said Evison. He was taking no chances. Then he said, 'Hove to.' There we sat, drifting in the water. The heat was tempered by a mild breeze, and it was pleasant to do nothing for the ten minutes it took the prau to come up alongside us. Evison beckoned me over and told me to fetch a musket from the armoury and go to the top main royal. 'If you see anything suspicious, take a pot shot. Don't be too careless though. If they're just merchants, I don't want to frighten them off.'

The prau grew closer. Both bow and stern were carved to a sharp, almost vertical, point and the boat was painted a beautiful blue and red. 'State your business,' shouted Evison when we were in hailing distance. There was only a scattering of men aboard the prau – at least on the upper deck. I thought perhaps there might be more in the hull and scanned their flanks for evidence of guns pointing at us.

Most of the crew wore only loincloths on their spindly bodies, but then a fellow wearing a fine silk robe emerged from a covered structure at the stern. He shouted over, 'Cloves, pepper. We trade for goods or money.'

Evison took his time replying. 'We'll come over.' Then he despatched Hossack to oversee the launch of the *Orion*'s cutter. I was summoned down from the mast and told to join the crew of one of our starboard guns. 'Bring him over here with a sample of his wares,' I heard the Captain say to Hossack. He was still being careful.

The merchant brought across two small barrels of goods. Evison and he greeted each other formally and I sensed a growing trust between them. Although a native, he spoke enough English to begin a lively conversation and goods were offered for sampling. I watched with fascination as Evison sank his arm into a barrel of spices, took out a handful near the bottom, and sniffed and tasted the wares. Maybe one day I would have the skill and experience he obviously possessed.

The Captain nodded and the merchant smiled. They haggled awhile, then the fellow called over to his ship. A few minutes later she was nestling up to our starboard side. While some of us stood by our guns, the rest of the crew helped to haul a dozen barrels aboard. Evison inspected each one, and seemed well pleased with this unexpected opportunity. The business was completed by mid-afternoon and the prau headed back to the bay.

I expected us to sail away, but Evison announced we would wait for the merchant to return with more of his goods. 'Fine nutmeg and ginger he tells me, and at a very favourable price.'

I supposed this was the way the Captain preferred to trade, away from harbour officials who might question his lack of licence.

'I don't want us getting careless though,' he warned. 'They can be a treacherous bunch these islanders, so we shall keep a full complement of men on the guns and take all the usual precautions. We shall stay here until midnight and then sail on if he doesn't return by then.'

It was a tense afternoon, sitting there waiting. In these waters it felt safer to be forever moving forward. Over supper the men echoed what Garrick had told us about the pirates here. When they attacked, they rarely left a soul alive. There were exceptions. 'I heard they sometimes just mutilate all that are still alive,' said Thomas Bagley. 'Cut their hamstrings or worse.' I was sick of this conversation and wanted to hear no more. But I knew Richard and I had made a bad start with our crewmates so thought it best to say nothing.

Bagley perked up. 'Now here's a juicy piece of tittle-tattle,' he said. 'I heard Hossack was captured by pirates in these waters a few years back. They stripped him naked and shaved his head.' Everyone laughed out loud at that indignity. 'Then they sold him as a slave. Lucky bugger was bought by a Chinaman who spoke English – he was a trader too. He set the Lieutenant free, worse luck for the rest of us.'

Bagley's story cheered everyone up. We went back to our duties feeling perkier. No wonder Hossack was feeling edgy.

The breeze dropped a little as the sun sank into the horizon. Night fell and the sky grew dark once clouds obscured the moon. The heat seemed to settle over us like a wet cloth, and the darkness around the ship took on a velvet, impenetrable quality. Another storm was brewing.

The passengers retired to bed, certain that they had seen the last of the day's excitement.

As we waited for the merchant's return, Hossack made his rounds far more frequently than every quarter hour. He and Evison were repeatedly found in deep discussion. Halfway through the evening Evison gave the command to raise the anchor. We would drift a little, to be sure, but he was preparing for a swift departure.

'What's keeping them?' said Richard, who was on night watch with me. He was anxious too. 'It's a calm night. The sea's as flat as a pancake. They should have returned by now.' He yawned loudly. 'I need my bed.'

To the east the sky began to rumble. 'Maybe they're afraid of being caught in a storm?' I said.

My suggestion hung unanswered in the air.

'Look, there's a light,' said Richard. 'They're coming back.' Half a mile away, a single lantern could be seen swinging through the night, its reflection clear in the water beneath the bow of the vessel that carried it.

'Good,' said Garrick. 'Let's hope this business is over quickly so we can be on our way. We need to make the most of these night breezes. They're often gone by daybreak and we'll find ourselves becalmed.'

As the light grew nearer, the storm did too. Thunder began to rumble ominously in the distance. I welcomed it. The rain would bring relief from the stifling heat. When the merchant ship was two hundred yards or so off, a flash of lightning away to the east fleetingly lit the sea around us. There behind the prau were two larger vessels. They were loaded to the gunnels with men, their scimitars and muskets outlined in an instant. 'They're pirates!' I shouted. 'There's two other ships coming.'

Evison turned at once and hushed me. 'Are you sure, Witchall?' he said.

'I swear it.' There was no mistaking the purpose of those dark silhouettes.

The Captain seemed unperturbed by this sudden reversal of fortune. I admired his courage, for I was already feeling frightened. I knew these pirates would not obey the rules of war and we would be fighting for our lives.

He stared into the emptiness. 'I can't see any other vessels, but if they're not carrying lights then we can be fairly certain they mean to do us mischief. Call all hands on deck and man the guns. Load them with grapeshot, every last one. Put word out to the male passengers. Anyone who can handle a musket should report to me immediately. I want this done as quietly as possible. We must make them think we know nothing of their approach.'

There followed a frantic five minutes of muffled activity. 'As soon as we fire our broadside we must make sail,' said Evison to us all. With only thirty men in the crew we would scarcely be able to reload before the pirates were upon us. Judging by the fleeting glimpse I had gained, we were terribly outnumbered. How I longed to be aboard a Navy vessel with topmen to attend to sails whilst the rest of us manned the guns.

We crouched by our cannons, staring through gun ports into the blackness, not knowing where our targets might be. 'They could be anywhere by now, those other ships,' said Richard.

Minutes passed. The light grew nearer – close enough for us to see the outline of the bow. Still we could not see the other ships. I began to doubt my own vision. Then the sky flashed again and there they were – two other vessels close behind the first. Plenty saw them that time.

Evison quietly issued orders to his crew. 'Lay your guns towards the light and wait for my command to fire.' Then he called out across the water.

'Vessel on the starboard bow. Declare yourself.'

A voice replied, 'Good captain. Is your cloves.'

They hadn't even bothered to get their story straight. We were expecting nutmeg and ginger.

'Why are the two ships with you not carrying lights?' shouted Evison.

'No two ships,' said the voice sharply. 'We come with cloves.' Then the light went out.

That was all the proof he needed. Evison drew his

cutlass and held it up. 'On my command, fire,' he said in hushed tones, 'then go at once to let down the sails.'

He waited only another few seconds, as men grunted and strained to shift the heavy cannons as best they could towards the general area of the approaching ships. This would be our one chance. The cutlass came down. The *Orion* shook with our broadside. Momentarily deaf from the noise, we raced up the ratlines to lower sail as fast as we could.

As my hearing returned, I could hear angry shouting amid the screams of the wounded. At least some of our shot had found its target. It felt as if we had stirred up a wasps' nest. 'Let's hope there's enough wind to carry us away,' I said to Richard. We could still not see behind us.

There, high up in the sails, I saw musket flashes from the praus and shots whistled past my ears. The handful of men on our quarterdeck returned fire. The *Orion* lurched forward as the wind filled her sails. 'All hands to the guns,' barked Evison into a speaking trumpet, loud and clear across the water. 'Grapeshot. Rapid fire.' He was bluffing. With so few of us it would take five minutes at least to reload these guns. But it might make the pirates think twice about getting close to us.

Then he beckoned his crew together. 'Just man the two starboard guns nearest the stern, and the two stern chasers. The more shot we can get off at them the better.'

The rain began to pelt down. The wind picked up. The

storm was coming closer but the elements were in our favour. Six of us manned the stern chaser on the larboard side of the rudder. Whenever we saw our quarry in a lightning flash, we fired a round of grapeshot. We were getting away and they had no big guns to punish us. We would have been done for though, if they had got close enough to board us.

We sailed on. I was glad we were on our way. If one lot of pirates felt safe enough operating in these waters, then who was to say there wouldn't be more. Ahead lay Coupang, where Evison had announced he would be going ashore, and Richard would be leaving.

For now, I was the hero of the hour. Seeing the pirates coming, I had saved the ship from a surprise attack. Several men who had previously ignored or jostled me clapped me on the shoulder to thank me. Something good had come of this encounter after all and in the days that followed there seemed to be a grudging acceptance of us among the crew.

CHAPTER 5

Peculs and Catties

I felt some trepidation when we first set eyes on Coupang. We had heard a lot about how dangerous these islands could be for sailors like us. But the settlement I could see looked safe enough to me. It was a small town, surrounded by palm trees behind, and with a forest of tall ships in the harbour, here to trade or resupply. Amid all this greenery stood a church, a fort and other European buildings. They looked out of place in the savage splendour of the landscape, dwarfed as they were by the mountains that surrounded the town. The natives had their own buildings in the foothills above. There were scores of little huts, fashioned in a beehive shape.

The forest shoreline looked familiar enough, but what lurked beyond the settlement? The closer we got to the shore, the hotter and stickier the air became. It drained our strength and teemed with pestilent vapours. I wondered about the alien creatures that lurked in the forest. Were the spiders and snakes as poisonous as the ones we had found in the bush of New South Wales?

Late on an overcast afternoon we lowered our anchor. There had been no downpour that day but the sky was swollen with rain. Purple light shone through the hazy clouds, giving the place a dream-like air.

Captain Evison announced we would go ashore the following morning. That evening, as the sun sank over the western horizon, I stood on the deck with Bel and Richard, watching a vivid sunset. Was Richard really going to leave us tomorrow? I couldn't quite believe it.

Purple and orange light filled the sky. The world felt utterly still. Bel said, 'Makes it all worthwhile, dunnit – all the rain and the seasickness and the awful food – seeing something like this. I never seen a sunset like this back in Bermondsey.'

'Did you talk to the Captain about going ashore?' I asked her.

She nodded but her mouth puckered into a pout. 'Mrs

Evison wun't 'ear of it,' said Bel, mimicking her Lancashire accent. '"More than my life's worth t'tek the risk," the Captain says. We're not giving up though,' she laughed. 'We're going to nag him to death about it!'

She went below soon after and Evison came over to us at the rail. 'I'm taking a small party ashore to meet the local merchants,' he said to Richard and me. 'I'd like you both to come with me.'

'But I'm intending to leave the ship, sir,' said Richard.

'I know,' said Evison. 'Come anyway – you've plenty of time to find an American ship. This'll teach you about trading here.'

'The sly old dog,' I thought. He wants Richard to stay, and he's letting him know he's valued. I was pleased he'd asked me too. He obviously thought we were worth a bit of his time and effort. I knew we could learn a great deal from someone with his experience.

When Evison had gone I said, 'You're not really leaving me on my own with this lot, are you?'

Richard's mind was made up. 'What's that line from the Bible you're fond of, Sam? "To everything there is a season . . ." Well my season in the British Navy, merchant or otherwise, is at an end. I'll be sad to leave you behind, and Miss Lizzie. I shall miss seeing her every day.

'Come with me, Sam,' he said suddenly. 'Or come over to visit when you can. My family would give you a job. We can sail ships together. You'll make your fortune there. We're not so bothered about what a man's station in life is. We take people as they come in Boston.'

It was a tempting thought.

Next morning Evison paid him off. Then we took one of the *Orion*'s smaller boats to the quayside, just the Captain, Richard and me. Although it took a while to get used to it, it was good to put my feet on solid ground again. Richard headed off, keen to find a ship to take him home. He promised he would return to say goodbye, but I watched him disappear into the crowded quayside with a lump in my throat, convinced I would never see him again.

'Won't we need more of us?' I said to Evison. 'Safety in numbers.'

The Captain shook his head. 'Natives round here are a pretty docile lot.'

They seemed quite lively to me and very different from the wild inhabitants of New South Wales. Although most wore little more than a linen cloth around their loins, they were clean and healthy and the children especially seemed bright and curious.

Evison had a few words of the local dialect and stopped to ask a young man directions. 'I've been here before,' he said to me, 'but I need a slight reminder of where to go.' The fellow disappeared, then returned a moment later with a pail of a slightly milky liquid. The Captain must have used the wrong words. He wasn't concerned. 'Try this,' he said handing over a coin, and offering me a small wooden cupful. It smelled sugary. I took a sip. Cool and sweet, it slipped down like nectar.

'Wonderful, isn't it?' said Evison with a smile. 'It comes from those palm trees. Lontars they're called.'

'Is it coconut milk?' I asked.

'No, they tap it from the trunk – collect it twice a day. I'd buy it to sell in London if it would keep. We'd make a fortune. But it won't travel.'

Ahead of us was a large, noisy crowd. As we drew nearer, I heard angry squawking. It was a cockfight. Evison stopped a while to watch, but I held back, not wanting to look. I saw enough to know the birds had blades attached to their legs. When I was a boy, I had kept three chickens – William, Mary and Matilda – and had grown to love them. As far as I knew, they were still alive in Wroxham. They were so tame they would come to the kitchen door and peer inside, waiting to be picked up. Then they would coo as I stroked their soft feathers.

This fight had drawn upwards of a hundred people. One bird eventually ran from the battle. But even then its torment was not over. The other bird was held before it. 'It's their tradition,' explained Evison, who had been too wrapped up in the fight to notice I'd turned away. 'The winner has to have enough strength left to peck the loser three times. Only then is he declared the victor.'

Evison found his bearings and we headed up a hill away from the harbour, then along a well-beaten path from the main settlement. The chief merchant here was a Dutchman and we soon arrived at his house. It was built in a native style, and was quite grand with a large straw roof and low walls, but light and spacious inside.

Waiting for us were several of the local chiefs. Unlike the almost naked people on the street, these men were dressed in beautifully embroidered waistcoats that stretched down to their knees. Their legs were covered by long cotton drawers, but none wore shoes or stockings. The room we entered was decorated in the native style, with little in the way of furniture but many plump silk cushions, bordered with fine gold and silver thread.

As the merchant made his introductions, the chiefs all put their hands together and lifted them to their head. This gesture, I was told later, was known as the salem.

We were offered a choice of coffee or toddy – a spirit distilled from palm juice. 'Have the coffee,' whispered Evison. 'The other stuff will floor you.'

Our refreshment arrived in fine bone china cups, decorated in the English floral style. This was the sort of tableware our village parson would provide for eminent visitors. It seemed strangely out of place in this exotic location.

I sat back to watch Evison negotiate. He had buckles, nails and cloth to sell, and from the start he made it clear that Spanish dollars were the only currency he would trade in. They started haggling over pepper. The merchant suggested twenty dollars per pecul. Evison offered ten and budged slightly to twelve. So it went on.

'Spice above any other item, Witchall. Any Captain will prefer spices. Try not to pay more than a dollar per catty. Good cinnamon will always fetch twelve to fourteen shillings a pound. Cloves a little more. Nutmeg less. Mace is more valuable, and you'll pay twenty to twenty-five shillings a pound for that.'

I listened, marvelling at these facts and figures, accumulated in a lifetime's trading. After Evison had inspected the goods, he bought several barrels of pepper, cinnamon and nutmeg. He marked each with an elaborate chalk signature over the lid and asked for them to be taken to the quayside ready for loading on to the *Orion*.

Then we were taken to another house further up the hillside to look at some cloves, which we were assured had been brought fresh from the islands to the north. 'They've a lot of them,' said Evison to me, 'and they're keen to sell at a generous rate.'

There were four barrels, and the lid was taken off one so we could inspect them. Evison picked them up and ran the small woody buds through his fingers. 'When you buy cloves they must feel slightly oily to the touch, leaving a little residue on the hand, and be easily broken.' He snapped one open and held it up to my nose. 'They smell fine, now place one on the tip of your tongue. It should taste hot, aromatic, so that it almost burns the back of your throat. A fresh clove has fragrance and yields a thick reddish oil when you squeeze it gently.'

Then, much to the consternation of our host, Evison put his arm into the barrel as far as it would go. He pulled out a handful and regarded them carefully. Then he shook his head. 'No, sir, we will not be taking these,' he said brusquely. We left with only the merest hint of a goodbye.

I asked him what had happened. 'It's an old trick the Dutch play,' he said. 'They put fresh cloves at the top of the barrel. But the rest are a mixture of fresh and distilled. They've taken them and extracted their juices – you can tell by their paler colour, shrivelled appearance and the fact that many have lost the bud on top. The Dutch sell their cloves by weight, so this makes them an extra profit. There's another trick they play where they soak them in water to make them heavier, but that's easy enough to spot when you squeeze them.'

When we returned to the harbour, Hossack had brought the *Orion* up to the quayside. I spent the afternoon helping to load spices into our hold, and making final preparations for *Orion* to leave Coupang. Richard had not yet come back and the thought of having to say goodbye to him lowered my spirits. Just as I was beginning to worry that I had missed his return when I was ashore with Captain Evison, I saw him hurrying down to the harbour.

I asked Evison for permission to go ashore to say goodbye. As I ran down to Richard, he caught sight of me and stopped in his tracks. He looked suitably solemn for such a sad occasion but as I came close his face broke into a great big grin. 'I'm not going, Sam,' he said. 'There's an American ship just sailed, and they say there might not be another for six months or even a year. I don't want to be stranded here that long. I'll pick one up back in London.' I cheered out loud and gave him a big hug. 'Here, steady on,' he said. 'I thought you British were meant to be reserved.'

We had one more stop before we could set sail for home – the port of Bencoolen in Sumatra. I asked the Captain what we might find there. 'Pepper – can't have too much pepper, and more nutmeg, cloves, hopefully good ones this time, camphor, timber – the most beautiful teak in the world, and dragon's blood.'

'So whose job is it to catch the dragons?' asked Bel.

Evison wasn't used to having his leg pulled. Perhaps he thought it was a serious question. 'It comes from the dragon's blood palm, lass. A very efficacious crimson powder. It'll cure the pox or the flux and you can even use it to colour your paints and plasterwork.

'There's gold here too – somewhere up in the heart of the island.' He looked over to the shore. Dense jungle began at the very lip of the sea, with just a short strip of sandy beach along the tide line. 'But there's headhunters too, and cannibals. So I wouldn't like to go to the trouble of finding it.'

Staring into that mysterious interior I felt a deep, almost overwhelming curiosity. Earlier we had sailed past steep mountains that plunged down into the water like the most formidable cliffs you've ever seen. I would go, I wanted to say, just to find out what was there. Headhunters with spears. Would they be any match for our pistols, muskets and cutlasses? 'We could come back here, maybe, when we're older,' I said to Richard. 'Go and search for that gold.'

From the ship, Bencoolen looked much the same as Coupang. Evison took me and Richard ashore again, but this time we came with six of the toughest-looking seamen on the *Orion*. 'There's plenty here who'll be out to rob us, so we'll need to have our wits about us,' said Evison. We all carried pistols and cutlasses.

They were quite a different kettle of fish in this port. The buildings here seemed to be in a poor state of repair and many of the natives dressed in filthy clothes and looked as though they never had enough to eat. These ragged people had a desperate look about them, and clamoured around us asking for money. I searched their faces, wondering who among them would turn on us when we refused them. I was extremely glad we had come as a gang.

'Most of them are slaves to opium. It's what they do instead of drink,' Evison explained as we walked through dirt-strewn tracks to the merchant quarter. We passed one beggar lying in the gutter. It was difficult to tell whether he was dead or alive.

'Don't go trying it, Sam, I beg you,' said the Captain. 'They say it's like the most wonderful dream you ever had, then you want to do it again and again and it enslaves you. The rich ones here, they're slaves as much as the poor. But they have money to pay for it and servants to run their homes and businesses. The poor, they live like starving beggars just to scrape together the money to buy some.'

Our visit did pass without incident, though I was glad to be back on the ship. It seemed strange to be among so many people with glazed, faraway eyes. Our trade completed and our hold full of goods, we sailed on along the island chain, heading for the Indian Ocean. So far, luck had been with us.

CHAPTER 6

Ten Little Daggers

There was an unnatural stillness in the sky – no seabirds circled our ship. They knew something bad was coming our way. The animals in our manger sensed it. The sheep and goats lay down in the straw, tense and wary. The hens on deck stopped clucking. Even Sydney stopped chattering. He kept flapping his wings trying to get away. I took him and his perch down below to my cabin and that calmed him.

Thunderstorms had come and gone all the time we sailed through the East Indies – they were just part of the climate here, along with the clammy heat and the occasional whiff of volcanic sulphur. The rain would come down in sheets, the sky would rumble and flash. Then, an hour later, it would be a breezy bright day again. But this one, coming over the horizon on our larboard side, seemed particularly ominous. The sky had the strange inky purple glow which seemed to be a feature of storms in these parts, and the moisture in the air was so dense you could taste it on your tongue.

Evison had us spend the day preparing for the storm. We brought down the canvas from the lower sails, then the lower yards too, leaving only the topsail yards and canvas to provide some control of the ship if we should drift dangerously close to the shore. It was a difficult job with this crew, lowering the heavy canvas and wood to the deck, and I was relieved when we had accomplished it without injury. The deck was cleared of all the birds and plants. Anything there that wasn't tied down was going to be swept away.

Night fell with such all-enveloping blackness I could have believed we had been cast into some purgatorial void. Then the ship was lit by a majestic flash of lightning, which spread across the sky like an upturned, bare, satanic tree. This was lightning I had never seen before – not white but blue.

That first bolt was our sign to go below – with only a handful of men on the weather deck left to stand watch. The hatches were battened down and all lights extinguished. Bel and Lizzie sought me out and we sat together in the dark. 'I've been in much worse storms than this,' I said, trying to reassure them. 'We'll be fine.'

Still, I muttered a thankful prayer that we were a good distance from land and only if the storm lasted several days were we likely to be driven ashore. I muttered another one too, beseeching the Lord to safeguard our wormy hull. If the timbers cracked open as we lurched between the waves, the ship would be lost with all hands.

Rain lashed the ship until the timbers were sodden, seeping down to the stinking hold, drenching every living thing, from bilge rat to Captain. We worked the pumps until our hands were bleeding and blistered, trying to keep down the rising water in the hold. Evison even enlisted the help of the passengers to take their turn. Some complained haughtily that they had paid for their passage and were not going to do the work of common sailors. But when Bel and Lizzie offered to do their share on the pump handles it shamed them into helping out. 'Come on, Mr Ellis,' I heard Lizzie say to one of the passengers, 'it will take your mind off the seasickness.' There was plenty of that too – making the dark, airless deck an even viler place to wait out this ordeal.

Then came the thunder, creeping nearer, an unseen menace, loud enough to shake the strakes from the hull. As the thunder passed over our heads, lightning split the sky so close I imagined the ship hit and shattered into a million pieces. Actually, this *was* worse than any storm I had endured before.

A rumble of thunder seemed to steal the air from the atmosphere and a blinding flash of light shook the ship from foretop to keel. We heard a creaking, splintering of wood and the braces and shrouds and ratlines shrieking in their posts. A brief silence followed. Then a huge crash rocked the ship from bow to stern.

One of the passengers screamed.

'That'll be a mast,' I said to Bel. 'I'm needed on deck.'

I was almost knocked off my feet by the force of the wind and drenched in a second by sheets of blinding rain. Gigantic waves towered above the weather deck on either side. I saw at once the mainmast had been struck close to the deck and toppled. The smell of it smouldering caught in my nostrils. Evison and the officers were out on deck, frantically trying to save their ship. The mast had fallen over the larboard fo'c'sle, mangling the rigging of the foremast and smashing one of the ship's boats. Now the topmost part of the mast lay broken in the sea, with the canvas on the upper yard soaking up water and giving it greater weight to drag the *Orion* down. The lower part stood crooked above our heads, trailing a tangle of ropes. Leaning over the rail, I could see the larboard gun ports perilously close to the waterline.

I seized a boarding axe and I began to hack away at the shrouds and ratlines still holding the upper mast to the ship. Richard and John Garrick joined me. Other men hacked at the mast itself, close to the rail. The three of us made quick work of the ropes, though I'll never understand how we managed to miss each other's flailing arms with our axe strokes. As we cut through, the mast splintered and the stout lower portion crashed down on to the deck. The remaining rigging attached to the upper mast was quickly severed and with a noticeable lurch the *Orion* raised itself in the water.

Now the lower mast rolled to and fro on the deck, threatening to crush any man who got in its way. William Bedlington came to join us. Never was I more pleased to see this hulking brute of a man. As we pushed our backs against the mast, a huge wave rolled before us across the deck. The water swept the mast and us along to the side of the ship, snatching our breath away. Soaked and spluttering out seawater I may have been, but I was grateful not to have been crushed against the rail or washed overboard. We heaved the remains of the mast over the strakes with a final, almighty effort. If we could safely ride out the rest of the storm, the worst of our troubles were over.

As we watched the mast drift away, Garrick said, 'That'll put another two months on our return. I hope we don't have to outrun any more pirates.'

Navy ships carried spare masts, but not the *Orion*. Evison spoke to him. 'We shall go ashore at the first opportunity and fashion ourselves a new mast. Plenty of trees close to the shore. You can choose one and we'll plane it down.'

When the storm had blown itself out, we sighted land on the starboard horizon. As we drew nearer, I looked over the dense green shoreline and wondered what lurked within. I was curious and I was apprehensive. Evison gathered us round to announce we would be looking for food and water as well as a new mast. 'There's plenty to do, so we'll be here a few days. We'll come back to the ship every night, though. I'm not leaving anyone on land after dark.'

What might we find ashore? Evison volunteered no information. Did he just not know, or was there something he didn't want us to know? I would ask at a suitable moment.

Close to the shore it did not take long to find a favourable spot and Evison launched the ship's cutter. With him were ten of the crew including myself and Bel, whose campaign to persuade the Captain to go ashore had finally succeeded. Lizzie wanted to go too, but here Evison absolutely refused. Bel was obviously of less concern, and the Captain made it clear I was responsible for her safekeeping. Richard had not volunteered to come. 'I had enough of the jungle in New South Wales,' he said.

The boat put down on a long narrow crescent of beach bordered by thick vegetation. Above us loomed the smoking summit of a tall volcano. A sharp, acrid smell pierced the air. There was another smell too – rotting human flesh. We found the bodies soon enough. There was a trail of them down to the shore. It looked as if they had been fleeing for their lives. The corpses were hideously burned and blistered. Evison shook his head. 'The volcanoes – they give off hot vapours, hot enough to kill anyone caught up in them. You can see them coming down the mountain, a big misty blob shimmering in the trees, which burst into flame as they pass.'

We buried the natives quickly in the sand. Bel joined in with the rest of us. I liked her for that. 'Every one deserves a burial,' said Evison. 'Even these savages.' Digging the graves wearied us all – the heat sucked the strength from our muscles.

While Evison and Garrick supervised the others in the finding and felling of suitable timber, Bel and me were sent into the jungle to look for fruit and fresh water with our shipmate Thomas Bagley.

'I should be good at this,' I boasted. 'After all that time in the bush in New South Wales.'

But this wasn't like the bush at all. It was dank and

dripping – a stultifying wet-dishcloth heat that had us all drenched in sweat in minutes. Still, it was a magnificent place, with tall trees reaching a hundred or more feet before their canopies opened to the sky. The flowers were big and their colours garishly bright. Here and there shafts of sunlight poured down like glowing waterfalls, illuminating the dead leaves and moss of the forest floor in dense pools of light.

My sense of wonder mixed with unease. Everything was too big. We were ants in a land of giants. Another foul smell caught my nostrils.

We followed our noses. In a forest clearing was the most grotesque plant I had ever seen. It had a flower wider than I could stretch my arms. The five petals had red and white stripes across them, like fat in meat. It stank like a rotting corpse.

'A place like this should be teeming with animal life,' I thought. It was here, all right, but we could barely see it. Once in a while, a flutter of wings would alert us to a bird flitting from one perch to another. Occasionally we would be distracted by a rustling in the bush, but other than the took-toka-tok call of the birds, all we could hear was the swish of our feet ploughing through the dead leaves on the forest floor.

I felt something slimy crawl up my leg – a slug-like creature, which I swiftly brushed off. 'Looked like a leech,' said Bel.

'Bet you wished you'd stayed on the *Orion*,' I said to her.

She laughed. 'Crikey no. It's nice to have a change of scenery. This is such a great adventure for me. We both kept pleadin' to be let off the boat. We could see the Captain weakenin' . . . It's Mrs Evison that wouldn't hear of it. 'Specially not Lizzie.' Bel started to mimic her. '"Much too dangerous for a young lady." I said to Evison, I've gone all the way to New South Wales and what have I seen? The inside of some of the posher houses of Sydney and the wooden sides of a ruddy ship. I want to have something more to tell about when I get home –'

An unearthly roar stopped Bel in her tracks. 'What the devil was that?' she said and gripped my arm.

Her fear was infectious. 'It sounded quite a distance away,' I said. 'But if it gets any nearer we'll climb a tree.'

Peering through the branches, I caught my breath and a shiver ran from the back of my neck to the base of my spine. Not twenty yards away was a tiger stooping down on its front paws to drink from a shallow river. Bel had seen him too.

Watching silently, I felt a growing sense of awe. I had never seen such a magnificent beast. He was about the same length as a cow, but much sleeker, stronger and lower on the ground. Having drunk his fill, he lifted his great head and sniffed the air. Everything he did seemed to be carefully calculated. He turned that head towards us, furry chops and whiskers still dripping with water. I wondered with growing terror if it was our scent he had picked up.

Further upriver, a flock of waterfowl made a noisy landing. The beast looked over at its leisure. Then it sauntered off at a lordly pace, muscles bulging on the shoulders and haunches of its sleek black and orange fur. It slipped slowly into the river with barely a ripple and began to swim towards its quarry.

We started to breathe again. 'It's a great big cat,' said Bel. 'I like cats, but you wouldn't want to stroke that.'

I had heard tigers ate people if they could catch them, but now wasn't the time to mention it. 'Let's get back to the shore,' I said, 'before it makes its way over here.'

We quickly gathered up our fruit and picked our way through the forest. I heard another terrifying roar and much squawking and flapping of wings. A goose or a duck wouldn't keep a hungry tiger happy for long.

'They say it roars before it pounces, to terrify its victims into paralysis,' I said.

'Shut up, Sam,' said Bel. 'The less I know about those things, the more I'll be able to keep putting one foot in front of the other.'

Going alone and unarmed into the jungle, we had

bitten off more than we could chew – something I suspected the tiger rarely did.

We heard a rustle in the bushes behind us and Thomas Bagley turned white as a sheet. 'It's coming back this way!' We stumbled through the undergrowth expecting the thing to pounce on us at any moment. I had seen its paws, and claws, and the thought of those sharp spikes digging into my back kept me running. Bel kept up as best as she could in her skirts. She was a good runner. Bagley lagged behind. He was a large rounded man and the heat was killing him. 'Wait for me!' he begged between gasping lungfuls of air.

Bel shook her head. 'Let's get up one of these trees. Something that big isn't goin' to climb trees, is it?'

We began to haul ourselves up the trunk of a tree with low branches, stopping when we reached a stout one about fifteen feet above the ground. Bagley was struggling for breath. 'This should be high enough,' he panted between great gulps of air. We sat down on the branch, legs dangling beneath us.

'Do we call for help?' I said. 'Will that bring the tiger to us? Or will it bring one of our shipmates who'll get eaten instead?'

'Let's just stay here for now,' said Bagley, 'and keep quiet. Maybe the thing will go away.'

I felt very thirsty. Bel passed me some of the berries

she had gathered and gave a few to Bagley. They felt sweet and juicy in my mouth – and balm to my swollen tongue. We calmed down a little. 'When we get back to the beach, I'm going to drink a gallon of water,' said Bel. Beads of sweat were dripping down her face and strands of dark hair were plastered to her forehead. 'And then I'm going for a nice long swim.'

Bagley shouted 'Here he iiiissssss . . .' In an instant the tiger had stretched out his body against the tree trunk and reached up with a paw to swat us. We all tried desperately to stand on that branch – none of us had expected the beast to have such a reach. In our fumbling haste, Bagley lost his footing and slipped. He grabbed urgently for the branch and for a brief moment he hung underneath. The tiger saw its chance and plucked him from the tree.

Bagley collapsed into a limp bundle. The creature grabbed the scruff of his neck and pulled him away. Whether Bagley had fainted in terror or had been stunned by his fall I didn't know. The tiger released its grip and sat on its haunches before him, as if wondering what to do next. Then it looked up at us. 'What are YOU going to do about it?' it seemed to be saying.

Bagley came to, sat up, then shrieked in horror. The tiger merely batted him down with a magisterial swipe and he lay there with the beast's paw on his back. 'This is MINE.' The tiger had its back to us, but I could see

Bagley breathing, his chest rising and falling rapidly. He was too terrified to utter a sound.

'What can we do?' said Bel.

I filled my lungs and yelled, 'HEEELLPP!!!' She joined me. Our cries echoed around the forest but there was no reply.

I searched around frantically, looking for something to use as a weapon.

'Sam, that creature will kill us both if we come down from this tree.'

Bagley tried to get to his feet again. The tiger pressed down harder on his back and gave out a tree-rattling growl. That seemed to drain the will from Bagley's limbs and he lay still.

I made up my mind. I stood on the branch and squeezed past Bel. There was a stripling branch above my head, and I began to wrench it back and forth in an effort to break it off.

'Are you mad?' said Bel in disbelief.

'I'm not going to watch him being eaten alive,' I said. I felt desperately at odds with myself. Was I being stupid?

'But Sam,' said Bel, 'what the hell are you going to do with that? Tickle him?'

Close by was a palm tree, its slender trunk arching up to a pinnacle of dense foliage. Skittering up the trunk, we saw a monkey wearing a little necklace. It was such a bizarre sight we both stared, mouths agape, almost forgetting the horror of the moment.

The creature returned an instant later with a coconut clasped firmly in one hand. 'Quick Bel, give me some of your fruit, let's see if we can trade.' She looked perplexed. 'Would *you* like to get hit on the head with a coconut?' I said.

We both shouted over to the monkey and held out a couple of cherries. A monkey wearing a necklace would be used to humankind. Sure enough the animal stopped in its tracks and slowly ventured towards us. The closer it got, the stranger it looked.

The creature was a brownish colour and the size of a small pig. Its expressive face was almost human and large eyes looked at us quizzically. Round its neck, twinkling in the light, was a beautiful string of precious stones. We held out some cherries and it edged towards us.

'How do we get it to hand over the coconut?' said Bel under her breath. 'And not drop it neither.'

We needn't have worried. It simply held out the nut for us to take, then sat palm open, expecting our fruit in return.

'He's been trained to do this,' whispered Bel.

We gave him the fruit and he sat with us on the branch to eat it. I began to slowly make my way down to the forest floor. 'Sam, don't,' said Bel. 'Try and get him from up here.' I shook my head. There was only one way to do this, and that was right up close.

Bel sounded desperate. 'He'll kill you,' she whispered hoarsely, trying not to draw the tiger's attention. 'You'll never get close enough. DON'T do it.' She was getting angry now.

The further down the tree I crept, the closer I was to mortal danger. Between me and the tiger lay maybe fifteen feet of forest floor. If I could make it over without breaking a twig or stumbling, then maybe the tiger would not hear me. I crept and crept, keenly aware of Bagley's pleading eyes watching my every move. Soon I was close enough to smell the catty stench of the beast. I felt some ancient terror in my bones, a fear quite different from that of battle. This was an enemy that would not understand 'I surrender'. Yet even now, as I crept towards it, watching its lean muscular back rise and fall with each slow breath, I could not help but admire its power and beauty.

I had taken every care not to step on a dry branch, and had moved as silently as I could, but the tiger had powers of detection way beyond human senses. Languorously, he turned his head round to look at me, showing no surprise when our eyes met. My heart was beating so hard in my chest I imagined it was its thumping that had given me away. I froze in both motion and body. I had never felt so terrified, even with a noose around my neck on HMS *Elephant*.

The tiger's steady gaze was mesmerising. The eyes were both beautiful and petrifying. A yellow band around the orb, then a wide jade-green swathe before the black dots of the pupils. When I looked into Sydney's eyes, or the cats' and dogs' I had known, I sensed an understanding, even an affection. Here there was no empathy at all. Just teeth and flesh, predator and prey.

The tiger stared with regal disdain, daring me to come closer. I stood stock still, clutching my coconut. I began to tremble with fear, a wave of shivering which I could not stop. I wondered if he'd let me walk away or would that be his moment to pounce? I could not bring myself to move.

The loud crack of a musket broke the spell. The shot whistled past my ear and sent a shower of bark and splinters down on the tiger's head. Startled, the beast gave a ferocious roar and leaped into the dense undergrowth. It was all Bagley needed. He staggered to his feet and ran for the tree. We both scrambled up, as swiftly as our limbs allowed. 'Quickly,' screamed Bel. Any second now I expected those claws to dig into my back like ten little daggers. I hardly noticed Garrick, musket in hand, climbing up beside us.

Only when we had all reached the safety of a higher branch did I dare look down. The tiger came back a moment later, fluid as quicksilver, pacing backwards and forwards at the base of the tree. Stretching up again, waving those paws. But this time we were out of reach. He roared and we recoiled from the stench of his breath. It was the kind of roar you could imagine starting an earthquake.

'You roar all you like, mate,' Bel shouted down. 'Roarin' won't do us no harm.' He turned his attention to her, looking her straight in the eye as he snarled.

'Lord Jesus,' said Garrick. 'Just look at the thing.'

'You saved my life, Mr Garrick,' I said.

'I heard you shoutin'. Didn't you hear me callin' back?' he said. We hadn't.

Garrick tried to reload his musket, but it was a difficult procedure balanced on a narrow branch, just out of reach of a man-eating tiger. Whenever he moved, the branch wobbled or creaked alarmingly. He gave up and fixed a bayonet to the muzzle instead. 'Just in case he tries to climb up.' Garrick seemed quite calm, and his courage gave me heart.

The tiger started licking a paw. Then he turned away from us, as if in a huff. Bel giggled. 'He's just like my Growler, back home. He sulks too, when he doesn't get his own way.' It was strange seeing this magnificent beast behaving like a house cat.

Bagley was too shocked to talk. Four streaks of blood matched four ragged tears in the back of his shirt.

His neck was raw and bruised where the tiger had dragged him along.

The monkey made a little squeak and held out his hand. We gave him more fruit and I gingerly stretched out my hand to stroke the back of his head. Much to my delight he shuffled up the branch towards me and put one of his arms around my back.

A few minutes passed. Birds erupted from the trees behind us. Something else was bumbling or prowling around. The tiger had grown bored. He strolled slowly back into the forest, searching for something less troublesome to have for his dinner.

We weren't ready to move. Anything could happen when we came down from that tree. But after a while we heard other voices calling for us, Evison's among them. Startled, the monkey bounded away.

'Over here,' cried out Bel, and soon enough Evison and three of his men appeared.

'What in heaven's name are you doing up there?' asked the Captain. When we told him, he sounded a bit affronted. 'You might have warned us,' he said.

Bel was unabashed. 'I knew you'd have muskets,' she chided, and went on, 'Mr Garrick here just saved our lives!'

We walked off, Bagley still too pale and frightened to talk.

'Just one thing,' said Bel to me when we were back on

the beach. 'The monkey. I wonder who gave him that necklace and taught him to fetch coconuts?'

Were there other natives here? Maybe he had been the pet of one of the dead we had buried. Maybe he had escaped from someone who was watching us even as we spoke.

CHAPTER 7

Company

I t took Garrick another day before he found a tree suitable to use as a mast. It was duly felled and laboriously heaved out to the beach where he set about stripping and preparing it for the ship.

We stayed there on the beach during the day and returned to the *Orion* at night. She was anchored a fair way off, for the sea was shallow for several hundred feet beyond the shore. Now, whenever I returned I kept thinking about who owned that monkey and whether they would make themselves known to us.

I asked Evison if he knew anything about the people

of these parts. 'A bit,' he said cagily. 'There aren't many of them, so I'm hoping we won't come to their attention. They're dirty in their dress and dwelling places, but they're clever too – they cultivate land, breed cattle and have their own script. They believe in evil spirits. They are small in stature – the women especially rarely grow taller than our ten year olds.'

'They don't sound too bad,' I said. 'They train monkeys too.' This was of no interest to him.

Then Evison said, 'Their least appealing feature is a fondness for human flesh. I don't think we should tarry here too long.'

That day I heard Evison and Garrick arguing. 'It'll not be ready for another three days,' said the carpenter crossly. 'I do a bad job and it'll come crashin' down in calm weather never mind a storm. I'll not have sailors' lives on my conscience.'

Evison was jumpy. Perhaps he felt we were pushing our luck staying this long. He often peered into the jungle close to the beach, as if he were expecting trouble.

Now when we ventured into the jungle to search for food and water we went in groups of four or five, at least two armed with musket and pistol.

Two days later the natives made their first appearance. Ten of them stood on the far edge of the sweeping crescent of sand that made up the beach. They were naked save for loincloths and leaned on their spears, broad brown faces regarding us blankly.

'They're all children,' said Bagley with derision. 'Just look at the size of them.'

'They might be small,' said Evison, 'but they can still kill us. They're sizing us up, wondering if we're worth a fight.'

He and Garrick fell into conversation. 'There's several days' work here that'll go to waste if we just up sticks and run,' said the carpenter. 'We don't know for sure that they're hostile. They might just want to trade?'

'Let's see then,' said the Captain. 'Men. Gather your belongings, but do it slowly. Don't let them think we're frightened of them. Let's see what these fellows are like.'

Evison turned and stood aside from the rest of us, then waved. One of the native men, attired in a fine feather headdress, stood forward and waved back. Then they called and beckoned Evison to come over to them.

'Don't go,' said Bagley. 'They could kill you on the spot and then have a go at us.'

The distance between them and our boat moored near the shoreline was roughly the same. We could not be certain of reaching it before they caught up with us.

I could feel the fear running between us like a magnetic force.

Evison was being put on the spot. 'Who will come with me?' he said tersely.

Not going would show we were afraid of them. 'I'll go,' I heard myself saying.

'I need brawn, lad,' he said.

My volunteering shamed the other men. Lieutenant Hossack, Garrick and Bedlington stepped forward. 'Are you all armed?' asked Evison. They nodded. 'Then let's see what they're made of.'

Seeing four of our party walk towards them, the native chief immediately selected three of his men to go with him, and they walked forward to meet our fellows on neutral ground.

As they grew closer the chief called out, 'Geen wapen.'

'That sounds like Dutch,' said one of our men. 'He's saying "No weapons."'

To emphasise the point the natives laid down their spears and knives in the sand.

We saw Evison and his men do the same with their guns, and I wondered if some of the natives would nip out of the forest to snatch them.

The two groups met, and both Evison and the chief made bowing motions. We were still anxious, but the meeting seemed to go well.

Evison returned with a smile. 'They want to trade. I said we would return tomorrow with plates and nails. They say they have gold to give us. Gold from the far hills.'

'So you could understand them?' I said. Evison shrugged.

'A few words. The chief, he speaks a little Dutch and so do I.'

The next day we returned. The natives did too. Evison had brought several bags of nails from the *Orion* and went with two of the crew to barter with them. I watched from a distance. The Captain was arguing heatedly. We held our breath, wondering if our comrades were going to be slaughtered.

The natives backed away and began to make contrite gestures – bowing and holding their hands in a submissive way. I began to breathe again and noticed my hands were trembling. Bel held tightly to my arm. 'Thought we'd had it then,' she whispered.

Evison returned to our party. 'They've no gold, so there's no nails for them. Their chief says he has sent men into the mountains for it and they'll be a few days. But I don't think they're really going to exchange their gold for a few nails. I think they're waiting for more of their kind to arrive, and then they'll have a go at us.'

He turned to the carpenter. 'They're very interested in your tools, Mr Garrick. I think the sooner you're away with your mast and tool bag, the better.'

'Then let's go,' said Garrick. 'We'll have to carry on shaping the mast when we have it in place on the *Orion*.'

Evison spoke again. 'I can't take you all, and the mast, right now. I want those of you remaining to spend the last hour or two here stocking up on any fruits and vegetables you can find. It'll be valuable work and useful in keeping the scurvy at bay. Stay together, stay away from the natives and stay close enough to the beach to be ready for us when we return. I've told them we'll be back for their gold but my guess is they'll attack if they think we're going for good. If some of us stay, they'll know for sure we'll be coming back.'

The Captain took Bel to one side. He looked solemn as he spoke and she nodded a few times. Then we all helped push the mast into the shallows and watched as they attached it to the stern of the boat with a rope. Garrick hauled his tool bag aboard and they started rowing for the *Orion*. The natives watched from the edge of the forest and began a strange little dance, stamping their feet and spears into the ground in unison. It was a menacing gesture. Evison's response – a friendly wave and a promise to return – seemed out of place.

A handful of us remained. I couldn't contain my curiosity. I asked Bel, 'What did the Captain say to you?'

'Told me he was sorry he couldn't take me back on the boat just now,' said Bel. 'Said he needed every strong man he could get to haul the mast on to the ship.' She seemed unconcerned. 'Fair enough, I suppose.'

Lieutenant Hossack was among us. Evison obviously hadn't forgiven his Lieutenant for the fight they had had that dark night. When the boat had sailed past hailing distance, he sat down in the sand. We looked at him expectantly for orders.

Eventually I spoke. 'Shall we all go together, sir, to look for fruit, or in several parties?'

He looked bewildered. To our surprise he began complaining about what we had been asked to do. 'Bloody waste of time,' he said sourly. 'Fruit for scurvy. What stuff and nonsense. It's *work* that keeps the scurvy from men's bones, not fruit.'

Then he turned to me and said, 'Yes, off you go, Witchall. Take whoever will come with you. I shall stay here and summon you when the boat returns.'

It seemed an unnecessarily dangerous thing Evison had asked us to do. But maybe he did it to take our minds off our predicament. Off we went, Bel, Thomas Bagley and me. Bagley carried a pistol so we had some defence against any man-eating animal, but we had only powder for one shot, and I feared that would be best used to defend ourselves from the natives. We found mangoes and figs close by and I took off my shirt to make a cradle to carry them.

When we'd gathered all we could we returned to the edge of the beach. Hossack was there, crouching where the jungle ended and the sand began. A small party of natives remained at the opposite end of the crescent beach. 'They've not taken their eyes off me the whole time you've been gone,' said the Lieutenant. I could hear the fear in his voice.

'We shall wait here until the boat returns. Then we shall run to it as quickly as we can. I dare say that will be the cue for the natives to attack us.'

'Why are they waiting?' I asked. 'Why don't they just kill us?'

Hossack shook his head. 'I don't know. Maybe they think they'll surprise us all at once. Maybe they hope to seize our boat. Maybe they're waiting for reinforcements. Maybe they're afraid of our guns.'

So we waited. The sun rose to its zenith and I was grateful for the cover of the trees. We slaked our thirst on the fruit we had found. Fear gnawed at my gut. Bel was frightened too. As she sat in the sand, she clutched her arms tight across her stomach and rocked to and fro.

We were sat slightly away from the others and I asked her if she was disappointed about having to leave New South Wales. I thought it would take her mind off the waiting. She was surprisingly forthright.

'I liked the place but I never liked the people Miss Lizzie mixed with. Lieutenant Gray was the worst and there were plenty similar. Hossack's a bit like Gray too. I keep waiting for her to see through him. That awful God-given arrogance. I never liked Gray. The first row

Lizzie had with him was about me. "You're far too familiar with that servant," he said. After that she'd be snooty with me when he was there. Like it was expected of her. After they got engaged he started to drink more heavily.

'I made up my mind that if she married him I was going to go. I wasn't going to spend the rest of my life being kicked up the backside by an oaf like that. Then one day she came home with a black eye and told me she was going to call off the engagement.

'Gray got steaming drunk and told her, right in front of me, that he knew people who would kill her for five guineas. I wasn't having that. I said "I know people who would kill you for nothing." That shut him up.'

The *Orion* was a good half mile out at sea, and we could see they were still hauling the mast on board. Meanwhile, Hossack was plotting our best defence. 'We must stay on guard for an attack at any quarter. The natives may decide to capture or kill us before our men return. They could come round under cover of the jungle and surprise us from behind.'

I looked over to the far side of the beach. They were still there, and I could swear there were a few more of them. A quick count numbered twelve. With ourselves and the men in the boat we would still just about out-number them.

Bagley held his pistol plainly in front of him. 'Don't fire unless you're sure of your target,' said Hossack. 'I have a pistol, but I have only powder for it and no shot.'

Every flutter of wings or snapping twig close by made us start. I counted fifteen natives now and perhaps more were creeping around the beach towards us. They stood plainly in view, leaning on their spears, staring over to where we sat.

We heard a clattering close by. Peering into the dense undergrowth we saw only dancing shadows. I caught a glimpse of a shoulder or an arm, perhaps ten yards away from us. Bagley must have seen it too for he fired his pistol into the forest. I saw a flash of orange fur as a monkey hurtled away. The whiff of gunpowder caught in my nostrils and when my ears had stopped ringing from the sound of the pistol I could hear laughter. Not close by, but from across the beach. The natives were amused by our behaviour. We had let them know how jumpy and frightened we were. Then they settled down and started to stamp their feet and spears again, as we had seen them do when the boat left.

'I don't think they're sneaking round to attack us,' I said. 'I don't suppose they'd be laughing if they thought we'd shot one of theirs.'

Now his last shot had gone, Bagley grew fretful. 'Why don't they come?' he kept saying. Hossack was unusually patient. He might be an ass, but he was proving to be a good man in a tight spot. 'The tide is against us. When it comes in, the boat will return. Now fill your pistol with powder,' he handed his powder horn over to Bagley. 'We might at least be able to frighten them with some blank shots.'

It was mid-afternoon when the *Orion*'s cutter started back towards us. 'Witchall, go and see if you can stand up and attract their attention somewhere where the natives can't see you,' said Hossack.

It seemed a forlorn task, but I retreated to the edge of the jungle and waved my arms wildly. The cutter headed close to our position.

It ran aground in the shallows, about ten feet from the edge of the shore, and Evison jumped out and waded towards us. So far, the natives had stayed where they were, but this was their cue. As soon as the Captain reached the beach, another ten of them emerged from cover and they all began to stamp their feet and beat the ground with their spears.

This was no time for clever tactics. 'Run!' shouted Evison, and we did. The fruit we had painstakingly gathered was abandoned and we hurtled along the beach towards the shoreline. The natives began to charge towards us and Hossack and Bagley both levelled their pistols and fired. At once, the natives threw themselves to the ground. It gained us several vital seconds before their courage returned and they raced forwards.

We reached the shore almost together, Bel running as fast as any of us, with her dress gathered up around her knees. But now stones were falling around us, and one hit me in the back of the head with such force it knocked me to the ground. I felt momentarily dazed but could hear Bel yelling, 'Get up, Sam,' as she dragged me to my feet. The spears would come next.

Men in the cutter were already pushing it out from the shore, and the boat was afloat by the time we reached it. Hands grabbed and bundled us aboard as stones rained down with merciless frequency. The fastest of the natives had already reached the water, and would be upon us any moment. Evison felled him with a pistol shot.

I remembered something I had read in Captain Bligh's account of his own battle with natives and shouted, 'Let's throw our clothes at them – that will distract them!'

Evison led by example. He took off his blue captain's jacket with fine gold embroidery and gleaming brass buttons, scrunched it into a ball and threw it over the heads of the nearest natives and towards the shallows. At once, some turned and scrambled back, determined to be the first to reach this choice prize. I threw my own shirt. Other men spun their hats. One man even hurled his precious shoes at them. Not all the natives were prepared to be distracted by our offerings. But as we began to scull for our lives towards the *Orion*, only a few still raced through the surf towards us. As it dawned on them they were now outnumbered, they stopped running. A last handful of rocks sailed over. In our confusion and haste to dodge them we failed to notice an incoming spear, aimed with deadly accuracy into the middle of our boat. Thomas Bagley was a target you could hardly miss. The spear hit him full in the chest and he lunged forward with a look of total surprise on his face, spitting blood over the back of the man at the oars in front of him.

'Hold him down,' said Evison heatedly as Bagley writhed in agony, 'before he does for us all.'

Bagley shrieked pitifully as Garrick pulled the spear out. Then Garrick held the poor man in a bear grip, lying him down as gently as he could in the bottom of the boat. 'Keep still, old mate, or we'll all be slaughtered,' he whispered.

'Put him over the side,' said Lieutenant Hossack. 'He's as good as dead.'

'We'll do no such thing,' said Evison. 'Now row for your lives.'

I had seen men with these sorts of injuries linger for days. Mercifully, Thomas Bagley did not live to see our return to the ship. He went a deathly pale and his legs began to tremble and after a few agonised spasms his body gave up the ghost.

CHAPTER 8

The Speckled Monster

We sailed through the oceans and the weeks merged one into the other. Our creaking ship braved the rigours of the sea and although men were frequently ordered to pump water from the hold, the *Orion* carried us through the Indian Ocean. Close to the Roaring Forties, we stopped briefly at the Cape to reprovision, then continued into the sluggish horse latitudes and doldrums.

As we approached the Equator west of Africa, there was no breath of wind for days on end. Our salty diet of dried meat and dried peas and beans produced a terrible thirst in us all, especially on days when the heat was so fierce it melted the tar between the planking. Our water supply was sufficient but it was brackish and foul, even after a red hot poker heated in the galley fire was plunged in to purify it.

This was the worst part of the journey – there were no hostile natives or pirates to distract us, no volcanoes . . . We all lapsed into a glazed-eyed lethargy. Evison tried to keep his crew busy but we were too weary to grow restless and mutinous. Once every couple of days, to prevent an outbreak of disease, vinegar was sprinkled liberally below decks and the ship was smoked out with sulphur fumes. The sour smells lodged in our throats and made our thirst worse.

Although it was often hard to tell, we were making progress. The crew had long forgiven Richard's and my initial arrogance but they remained fellow travellers rather than friends.

The hull held, despite the attentions of the teredo worm, although John Garrick was firm in his opinion that once home the *Orion* would be unfit for another deep water voyage. Even the mast Garrick had fashioned from the tree trunk stayed in place. Evison was wise enough not to employ its full complement of sail, but it supported the yards we placed on it well enough.

What did fall apart was Lizzie's friendship with Lieutenant Hossack.

I overheard them talking one afternoon on the quarterdeck while I was taking a turn at the wheel. Lizzie absently asked him which ship he had sailed on before the *Orion* and he smugly told her he had been First Lieutenant on a slaver – the *Salamander*. 'We prided ourselves on only losing a quarter of our cargo,' he swaggered. 'The British slavers are the most humane in the world.'

Lizzie looked disgusted and Hossack bristled with righteous indignation. 'Come now, girlie,' he blustered, 'these Sambos are fair game. They're prisoners from their own little wars. The chieftains and princelings who trade in them would kill them if we did not take them.'

Lizzie was trying hard to rein in her indignation. 'And is it true that each of these poor men and women is chained for the whole voyage and that they have so little space in the hold that some are forced to lie upon each other?'

'They are hardly men and women like us, Miss Borrow,' said Hossack. 'Barely more than animals. If you saw them, you'd no doubt agree.'

'I have to say, Mr Hossack, that I am a great supporter of Mr Wilberforce and his abolitionists.'

Hossack's mask slipped. Perhaps it was the heat which made him so intemperate. 'Mr Wilberforce is an interfering do-gooder. Slavery is a blessing. The African is incapable of living as a free man. I'm sure you will know your Bible, Miss Borrow, and I can tell you that slavery is sanctioned from Genesis to Revelation. *"Cursed be Canaan. The lowest of slaves will he be to his brothers."* It's there in Genesis. Plain as daylight. Ye'll know good Christians believe that Canaan settled in Africa.'

'Mr Hossack,' said Lizzie sternly, 'I am unshakeable in my belief that slavery is contrary to the laws of God and the rights of man.'

Hossack's blood was up. 'Rights of man! Are ye referring to that subversive document by the traitor Tom Paine?'

Lizzie sighed. 'Mr Hossack. Perhaps we should restrict our conversation to lighter matters in future, such as the clemency of the weather and the progress of the *Orion*. We still have a long journey ahead of us. It would be so disagreeable to spend the rest of it in perpetual enmity.'

There at the wheel I was trying so hard not to snigger I nearly burst a blood vessel. I couldn't wait to tell Richard. It brought him a little glee and happiness when the rest of us were at our lowest ebb.

By late August of 1803 we could sense the days were getting shorter and colder. The journey had taken much longer than we had hoped but now at least we were back again at a latitude that chimed with our childhood memories of summers and winters.

Lizzie and Bel remained our good friends and I knew I would miss them when the voyage was over. Richard told me he had half a mind to ask Lizzie if she wanted to come back to Boston with him. 'It's the perfect time,' he said. 'If she says no, then I'll never see her again!' I knew she wouldn't go, but I didn't know whether she would be touched by his proposal or amused by his audacity.

Lizzie was the first of the passengers to spot the English coast. 'We're home! We're home!' She ran shrieking down the deck to drag Bel out of their cabin. There it was – Lizard Point – on the southern tip of Cornwall. Here were people who looked like us (but not as weather-beaten), and talked like us (though not as coarse nor spouting those sailors' words that were double Dutch to landlubbers), and more than likely thought like us too.

I had such a lump in my throat when I saw the first of England, I wanted to cry with joy. But there was a rage there too, at the injustice of our transportation, which had not entirely gone away. I shook those thoughts from my mind. There was so much I had seen and done on this extraordinary voyage. Wasn't that what I had wanted from a life at sea?

My thoughts turned to my home village of Wroxham. I had been so keen to escape that little piece of Norfolk that I had chosen the most dangerous occupation open to me. I had mixed feelings about going back. I did not know what I would find there. My childhood sweetheart Rosie, what had happened to her? Were my mother and father and brother Tom in good health, or even still alive? I had heard from them only once during my stay in the penal colony. I had written back telling them what a wonderful place it was – that was before things went wrong. I wrote again just before we left, telling them of our pardon. I had been assured the letter would be carried alongside official despatches and delivered in as little as six months, certainly faster than we would make it home.

I didn't want to go back to live in Norfolk, but I did long to stroll down those leafy lanes and see the joy on my parents' faces when they first set eyes on me. The wood smoke and polish smells of home filled me with a sweet, almost painful, longing. To have my meals lovingly cooked by my mother, rather than some cursing, peg-legged cook, who probably spat in the stew, would be something to look forward to. To stay in bed past seven o'clock and wake to breakfast rather than several hours of scrubbing the decks – that would be marvellous too.

We were five miles off the Dorset coast when we saw them. Four souls adrift in a small boat – two men of middle years, a young woman and a child of three or four. Judging by their clothes, they were people of some standing.

'Hove to,' shouted Evison as soon as the boat was spotted, and we put the *Orion*'s cutter over the side and rowed over. What could have happened to these people? They all looked shocked and bedraggled. The child and one of the men were wrapped in blankets. We towed their boat alongside and hauled them up. It was a novelty to see these new faces after so long at sea with the same people. Lizzie and Bel were up on deck and went at once to assist the ailing members of the party.

Evison came over. He spoke sharply. 'Two of you are feverish. Why are you adrift at sea?'

'Our ship was attacked by a privateer,' said one of the men. 'As passengers we demanded to be put over the side and allowed to escape. My companion and the child became ill while we drifted at sea awaiting rescue.'

The man was ill at ease, and would look no one in the eye. Evison was swift to smell a rat. 'No captain would give up one of his boats before a battle, nor set four of his passengers on to a vessel none of them knew how to handle. Tell me why you are adrift here, or you'll return to your boat forthwith.'

The man began to huff and puff. 'You doubt my word, sir? I'll have no man speak to me so insolently!' For a second I thought he was going to strike the Captain. I was glad to see he did not carry a sword.

Evison was unimpressed. 'I'm Captain of this ship, and while you're on my vessel, I'll talk to you how I like.'

But the man would not be cowed. 'We are travelling to visit Lord Hatherley in Salisbury and I'm sure he will be most displeased to hear of our disgraceful reception.'

Evison grabbed him by the scruff of the neck and dragged him over to the rail. 'Are you a good swimmer, sir? You'll need to be to reach the shore. Now tell me why you are adrift . . .'

The woman suddenly spoke up. 'Tell them, Burnley. It is wicked not to.'

The man spat his words towards her. 'I shall not be a party to my own destruction. You tell them, and you take the consequences.'

We stood agog, waiting to hear what she would say.

The woman looked up and spoke in a quiet, firm voice.

'It is true we were travelling by sea to visit Lord Hatherley. But a number of the crew were stricken by smallpox soon after we left Poole. The Captain is in the employ of Lord Hatherley, which is why we managed to persuade him to set us off so as to escape the disease.'

Watching her talk, I could imagine the arguments that had gone on in the boat as we sailed towards them and I admired her courage. She went on, her voice faltering in her distress.

'Alas, for my son, and Mr Curzon here, we appear to have left too late. I am sorry we have burdened you with our troubles.'

These words were like a curse. Everyone moved away from the castaways as she spoke. Lizzie and Bel silently and gently laid their patients down on the deck.

Evison spoke in a tone that invited no discussion. 'You will return to your boat at once, all four of you. My men will tow you to the shore, and there you must seek assistance.'

'But that is outrageous,' said the man. 'The child is especially weak. You are killing him.'

'You, Mr Burnley, are trying my patience. If any of my crew or passengers contract this illness, I shall hold you responsible. Now leave my ship before I put a pistol to your head.'

They clambered back in the boat, the woman clutching the child, the man holding on to his companion. Evison turned to the girls. 'Miss Borrow and Miss Sparke, you will go at once to your cabin and wait there until I say. You will touch no one nor stop to speak to them. For the moment you are under quarantine.'

They went, moving in a shocked and distraught way, and everyone hurried away from them as if they were lepers. Bel turned to me and I saw a haunted, pleading look in her eyes.

All hands were summoned on deck. 'Our visitors were infected with the smallpox,' said Evison. 'Those of you who have had this disease or who have been inoculated against it will gather on the starboard side. Those of you who have had neither the illness nor the inoculation will gather on the larboard side.'

It was a tense moment. I was relieved to see that most of the crew joined Richard and me on the starboard side, including those who had helped the castaways on board. Only a handful went to larboard.

'You men on the larboard side will confine yourselves to the larboard crew cabin in the bow. There's little risk you'll contract the disease, but I don't want to take any chances. I shall inform you as soon as I feel it is safe for you to join the rest of the crew.'

I said to Richard, 'What's going to happen to Bel and Lizzie?'

He shook his head. Then he said, 'They might be lucky. They might not get it. They should have been more careful.'

'When did you have your inoculation?' I asked.

'I didn't,' said Richard. 'I had what they call variolation. It's like inoculation only more dangerous. It's pretty barbaric. They blow dried smallpox scabs up your nose. They say one in fifteen die from it. But in Boston one in four die from smallpox, so it's worth the risk.'

Smallpox had visited my family when I was six. No sooner had the outbreak touched Wroxham than Tom and I were sent to our friends in Lowestoft. My two little brothers were too young to travel – both could barely walk and my mother was convinced she could keep them safe. She was wrong; they both died. My mother said their little bodies had been covered in horrible pus-filled spots. Soon after, our village parson told my parents he was to be visited by a physician called William Woodville, who would bring with him a cure. We two boys, and several others in Wroxham, were inoculated.

The crew of the *Orion* were edgy. They began to talk about what this evil disease had done to their loved ones and friends. 'The speckled monster,' said William Bedlington. 'It's an affliction to make the devil proud. My mother caught it and the spots all joined together and her whole body were one mass of suppurating poison. She died quick but some linger for days. It's a cruel malady.'

Richard and I went to talk to the Captain. 'What will happen to Miss Borrow and Miss Sparke?' I said.

Evison sighed. 'We don't know yet whether they'll fall ill. Sometimes the smallpox carries and sometimes it doesn't.'

Then he shook his head. 'Look, I've had several of the crew come and tell me the girls should be cast adrift in one of the boats. I know they both swim, and they could row to shore, especially if you and Richard took them, but it's not right abandoning them like that. I think we should keep them here to look after them. Mrs Evison and myself have both had the smallpox. She's offered to care for the girls if they fall victim to it.'

I felt a surge of gratitude to Mrs Evison. She had been the butt of our jokes for much of the voyage and none of us had liked her much, but she had a good heart. 'They'll stay in their cabin, 'til the illness develops or we know for certain it's passed.'

'Can we go and talk to them?' said Richard.

'No,' said Evison. 'You might spread the disease yourself if they have it.'

'Can we write to them?' I said. 'Keep their spirits up?'

'Yes, but you'll have nothing back from them. If the disease spreads, we'll be quarantined for months when we get to London.'

After several days, the girls were bored and Mrs Evison persuaded the Captain to let us go and talk to them through the door. 'You can't see them face to face. Don't get close.'

Mrs Evison stood at the door. Richard and I stood behind a rope she had placed on the deck, beyond which we were forbidden to step. 'How are you both?' I asked.

'We're worried,' said Bel. 'Neither of us has had the smallpox or the inoculation.'

'I often asked my mother if we could be treated,' said Lizzie, 'but her sister had her family variolated and two of the children died. I wondered if the problem lay with the physician and his method rather than the process itself, but Mama would not be persuaded. Now here we are in this terrible limbo, waiting for the signs . . .'

'My father wouldn't hear of it,' said Bel. '"I'm not having that mumbo-jumbo. It's not natural." I tried to get it done myself, but I never had enough money to pay for it.'

'Don't worry about us,' said Lizzie, sounding like she was about to burst into tears. 'We've got a porthole in our cabin and our books and each other for company. And Mrs Evison is bringing us our meals and everything is going to be fine.'

All we could do was wait and see.

Later that day we spoke to Captain Evison. He talked about the disease – almost as if he were a physician. 'I can't afford a surgeon for most of my voyages, so I've learned the hard way how to treat them who fall ill.'

'We need to wait two weeks. If the girls do sicken, then they'll have a fever then a rash. The rash'll spread and blisters'll form. If that happens the girls will be too ill to walk and even talk. That's when we find out if they live or die. There's one in three who get it die. And those that survive are often badly scarred.'

I could see he had the scarring himself. 'Sometimes, the scars are mercifully slight. Sometimes they're worse.'

As we sailed along the south coast of England, time seemed to slow down. If we felt like that, occupied in our work, how much slower the time must be passing for Lizzie and Bel, when they would fear every twinge of nausea or headache.

'Could we let them have Sydney for company?' I asked the Captain. 'They could teach him some new words?' He shook his head.

'Mrs Evison has got enough on her plate without having to clean up after that bird. And if the girls do get ill, the creature's squawking will only add to their torment.'

We visited when Mrs Evison allowed, but standing at a safe distance while she stood by the door did not make for flowing conversation. The girls were now sunk in deep lethargy. 'I never realised how long you could sleep during the day,' said Bel. 'Yesterday I slept for most of the morning and half the afternoon and then most of the night. Now I've woken with a crushing headache.'

A tight little knot twisted in my stomach. 'You need some fresh air,' I thought, but it seemed such impractical advice I said nothing at all.

CHAPTER 9

Quarantined

Next day Mrs Evison opened the door a crack when we came. I could tell at once from the look on her face that something had happened. 'The girls have taken bad,' she whispered. 'Both of them have a fever. Don't come back until the Captain tells you it's safe.'

Richard and I both went to sit at the fo'c'sle. 'Could be anything,' he said. 'Could be some of the swill they've had to eat.' We had not taken on fresh supplies since Cape Town.

'Then let us pray that's what ails them – that and lack

of fresh air and exercise.'

The Captain kept us informed. 'It's smallpox for sure. Mrs Evison and I have seen enough cases to know.'

First there was the raging fever. Then came the rash. Then both girls hovered in and out of consciousness. Then came the boils.

'But don't give up hope, boys,' said Evison. 'I've seen this illness at its worst. It's not flat black pox, and it's not the haemorrhagic pox, thank the Lord. Both of them are guaranteed to kill.'

'What the hell are those?' said Richard. I didn't want to know.

Evison explained. 'The first turns the skin black, then it's shed, like a snake or lizard. The other one's even worse. Black blood oozes from every orifice.'

We gave him two more letters. 'Keep them, lads,' said Evison. 'The girls can't even understand simple conversation right now.'

'Can anything be done to ease their suffering?' asked Richard.

'Mrs Evison is doing everything she can,' said the Captain. 'She's sponging them down with wet towels, and treating them with the steam inhalation when they are conscious and lucid. We have boracic lotion for the eyes and borax for the mouth, to lessen the effects of the blisters in those tender regions.'

'How long does this stage last?' I asked.

'We shall know the worst of it by the end of the week.'

By now we had rounded Broadstairs and Margate and were sailing up to the Thames estuary. The men who had not been inoculated were released from their cabin. No one else had contracted the disease.

Evison announced we would head for Chatham where the ship would be held in quarantine for several weeks until the authorities were sure the outbreak had run its course. What should have been a joyous homecoming was turning into a nightmare.

I passed the girls' room from time to time, and would pause outside, but never for long because there was a sickly sweet stench about it. I knew this was characteristic of the illness. I wanted to call Bel's name, but feared I would wake her from her rest. If she was asleep, then I wanted her to remain undisturbed.

As we approached our mooring downriver from Chatham dockyards, Evison summoned Richard and me to his cabin. He looked solemn and I knew he had grave news. Who would it be, Bel, Lizzie or both of them?

'I'm sorry to tell you that Miss Borrow . . .' I didn't hear the rest. I was just so relieved it wasn't Bel. Then I felt bad, for Lizzie was my friend too. Richard looked shocked to the core.

I started to hear again some of what the Captain was saying: '. . . her passing was a blessing . . .' 'suffered terribly and had already lost her sight' 'affected far worse than Miss Sparke'.

'And how is Miss Sparke?' I asked.

'Mrs Evison says the worst is over. I can tell you now she seems to have fought the disease and suffered far less from the blistering. We're hoping she'll be back on her feet in a couple of weeks.'

I put a consoling arm around Richard. We walked out of the Captain's cabin and stared blankly over the side of the ship as the fields and mudflats of Kent slowly drifted by. This was home, up close enough to see people in hailing distance on the river bank, cows, sheep, horses and carts, riverside houses and taverns. I should have been excited, but I just felt empty.

'She wouldn't have wanted to be blind and disfigured,' Richard said. 'She must have been admired for her beauty since she was a little girl. She spent her whole life entering rooms and houses and turning heads in admiration. It would have grieved her to look like that.

'I didn't really think she'd come back to Boston with me. But I had a faint hope. I would have asked her, right at the very end of the voyage. Poor Lizzie. What a terrible way to die . . .'

I had not seen him cry since the day we were sentenced to hang at Copenhagen and now tears streamed down his face. We had always talked about his attraction to Lizzie in a light-hearted way. His feeling was deeper than that. I too shed a tear at that moment. For my friend Lizzie and for Richard. Lizzie was the first girl he had fallen for. Who could have guessed it would end like this?

Lizzie was given a quiet funeral, with just Richard and myself and the Captain and his wife present. 'I don't want the whole crew gathered close round. There's still a small chance that others may develop the disease.'

Her body was wrapped in canvas, weighed down with three cannon balls, and set over the rail just as the sun reached its highest point in the sky. 'Beautiful day for a picnic,' she would probably have said. It was too. One of those lovely September days, just before autumn comes to take the warmth from the sun.

I kept thinking of the first time I saw her – two years ago as a passenger on the *Euphrates*, sailing out to New South Wales. She had this fresh beauty about her and was bursting with a zest for life. But now the world continued to turn and she was no longer there.

'Can I visit Bel?' I asked. I suddenly felt a great need to see her. She'd be very upset. She was shrewd enough to know how useful Lizzie was to her, but she had also been her best friend.

'You'll have to wait,' said Evison. 'Just be grateful she's still alive. You can write her a letter. She's probably strong enough to read it now.'

* * *

The ship settled into its quarantine routine. Evison insisted on running the same watches and kept the crew busy cleaning and repairing the *Orion*. The men grew bored and resentful, and I longed for the day when I could be rid of them.

Some of them took to gambling, despite the fact that the Captain had always forbidden it. When one man was injured in a knife fight over a gambling debt, Evison had the perpetrator flogged. It was a low point of the voyage, having the crew assemble to witness punishment on a grey autumn day, with a biting wind whistling in over the estuary. There was no more gambling after that.

A week later, I was summoned to see Bel. 'Don't touch her, don't get too close to her, but you can sit at her bedside,' said Mrs Evison. 'Come after eight bells on the afternoon watch.'

I feared what I would find almost as much as I had feared battle or storm. As I approached the cabin, I felt I was in a bad dream.

I knocked and a weak voice croaked, 'Come in, Sam.'

There she was, her face white and gaunt and her body all bones beneath the sheets. There were still some livid spots on her face but they were healing and the scabs had fallen off. Mrs Evison had done a fine job cleaning the room for visitors, but the sickly sweet stench of smallpox still hung in the air.

She gave me a weak smile. 'Don't come close, Sam,

don't risk your life.'

I told her I had been inoculated. She became terribly angry. 'My stupid, stupid parents. If only they had sent me . . . it wouldn't have cost them much, less than a couple of bottles of port, and I could have been spared all this.' She began to weep, choking back tears. It seemed to exhaust her.

'Don't touch me, Sam,' she cried. 'I still hurt all over.'

'I've been lying here these last few days wondering how this could have been avoided. When Lizzie saw the sick people, she said we should go to them at once. I agreed without a second thought. We didn't think, did we? I can't blame her for that. But something is bothering me.

'Did we both get it when we went to help the sick people when they came on board? Or did she get it and give it to me? Or did I get it and give it to her?'

'Who can tell?' I said, stuck for something to say. 'But you've been looked after well.'

'Evison should have kept us apart.' She was getting angrier. 'It was wrong to keep us both in our cabin. Maybe I would have just had it, and Lizzie would still be alive. Maybe she would have had it and died anyway, but I would have been spared.'

The effort to talk exhausted her. She stayed silent for a while then tears filled her eyes. She had obviously been brooding in her lonely cabin. Much as I liked the

Captain, I could see she had a point.

'Pass me a mirror, Sam, there's one in the drawer there.'

'Leave it 'til later, Bel,' I said. 'You look fine – you're thin and pale, as you would be, and you have some marks on your face, but they'll fade in no time.'

'Quick, Sam, quick, I'm begging you.' She was getting upset again. 'Mrs Evison won't let me look. I want you to help me.'

I fetched a small hand mirror and held it in front of her face.

She began to sob.

'No man will ever want me now.'

'That's not true,' I said.

She would not be consoled. 'And what am I going to do with Miss Lizzie gone? Who's going to take me as their maid with these hideous scars . . . I'll have to work for some bad-tempered harridan who'll want a plain maid to make herself look better.'

I came to see her again the next day, but her mood was much the same. She found fault with everything I said and sent me away after a couple of minutes. The next day, I thought she might want to pass the time writing to her parents, so I brought pen, ink and paper. She threw them to the floor, staining the deck and her sheets with the black ink. 'What am I going to say?' she wailed. 'This is what happened because you wouldn't have me treated! Go away, Sam Witchall, and don't come bothering me with stupid ideas.'

I left it for a week. I knew people behaved badly when they were tormented by grief and anger. But when I returned she wouldn't see me.

On 15th November, 1803, we sailed into London. It loomed in the distance – the great curving dome of St Paul's Cathedral, all those spires, and a huge mass of buildings and smoke – like a great shadow cast over the earth. This was a journey I had been longing to make since I first went to sea. I had heard so much about the city from my fellow sailors and now I was about to see it for myself.

By the time we reached the grand palaces and buildings of Greenwich, the river bank was crowded with houses. Richard had kept to himself in the days following the funeral, but arriving here seemed to perk him up. He pointed up at the splendid observatory atop the hill overlooking the river. On its roof was a large red ball mounted on a long pole. 'That gets hoisted up and dropped every day at twelve o'clock sharp,' he told me. 'All the ships in London set their chronometers by it.'

We sailed into the Pool of London, past the turn in the river at Limehouse Reach. The city looked like some vast human hive. Up in the topsails I could see how enormous it was and I was eager to walk those streets.

On the east side of the river we passed a gigantic building that receded almost as far as the eye could see. 'That'll be the warehouses for the new West India Docks,' said Garrick. 'They were buildin' that when I sailed out of here. They say it's the biggest buildin' in the world.'

We moored along a crowded quayside close to London Bridge. The Captain, it was whispered with a knowing smirk, knew exactly which dockside officials would be open to a bribe. They would turn a blind eye to his lack of a trading licence for his East India goods.

Evison paid us off. 'You can sail with me any time, Witchall. You too, Buckley. You've been a credit to the ship.' He wrote down his London address and told us to come and visit him if we were looking for work. Then he gave us our wages – over twenty pounds. It seemed like a fortune. 'Don't spend it all on drink and doxies,' said the Captain. 'And keep it well hidden about your person. Those streets are full of cut-throats and pick-pockets. One final task. I want you to deliver Sydney to his new master. I think it would be best for you to take him.'

I was happy to do him that favour. Evison was a good man and I would be proud to sail with him again. I didn't want anyone else taking Sydney to a strange new place either. I knew he would be confused and frightened by his unfamiliar surroundings.

We said our farewells to Mrs Evison, John Garrick, and the rest of the crew, even William Bedlington. I didn't want to see most of them again, but I wished them well. After a bad start we had finally learned to rub along with each other. To Garrick, at least, I owed my life. We made small talk about our plans. Most were going to spend a few weeks or months ashore, regaining their strength before they took their life into their hands on another voyage. It was a precarious existence, being a sailor, but there was nothing else to rival its excitement for an ordinary working man.

There was one last farewell to make. I went to Bel's cabin and knocked on the door.

'Who is it?' came a sharp voice.

'It's Sam, come to say goodbye.'

'Goodbye then,' she said, without even opening the door.

London Calling

We marched down the gangplank both carrying a small bag of possessions. It was precious little to show for our time on the other side of the world. Sydney perched on my shoulder and I felt like a pirate. He wasn't going to fly away in this strange town – but I had him on a long tether just in case.

'First things first,' said Richard, 'a mutton pie and a pint of ale.'

'A nice crusty loaf with fresh butter, and thin slices of beef,' I said.

'An apple and blackberry pie with custard,' said

Richard. As we strolled along the riverside, we fantasised about all the fresh food we'd find on dry land. 'Carrots and greens, straight from the fields.'

We sat down in the window of a riverside tavern and I felt a great surge of joy and relief. 'Here's to us, Richard, and here's to sitting here in a London tavern, rather than slaving away on Charlotte Farm for another five years.' I shuddered to think of how our lives would have turned out if our friend, Midshipman Robert Neville, had not arranged for our pardon.

'We've got letters to write,' said Richard. 'Not least to Robert and his father.'

'I must write home, and so must you,' I said. 'But I don't want to go back just yet, I'd like to stay here with you until you return to Boston.'

'Good,' said Richard. 'First we need lodgings. I propose we live like gentlemen for a month or so, and spend some of our money having a wild old time.'

'Done!' I said, and we chinked our pint glasses together.

First we had to deliver Sydney to his new owner. Captain Evison had given us directions to Bedford Square, in the district of Bloomsbury. Lord Montague lived in a grand town house there, which we reached after an hour's brisk walk. I couldn't believe you could walk for an hour and still be in the middle of all this bustle and mayhem. It took a few minutes to walk from one end of Wroxham to the other.

We rang the bell on the imposing black door to be greeted by a liveried footman. 'We've brought a cockatoo for Lord Montague,' I explained. The footman looked amused, then baffled, then severe. 'Be gone, you urchins,' he said and slammed the door.

We rang again. 'But we have. It's from His Excellency Sir Philip Gidley King, the Governor of New South Wales. Please tell Lord Montague we're here.'

'I'll do no such thing,' said the footman. 'But you may hand the creature over to me.'

Sydney flapped and squawked and the man recoiled. 'He's quite nervous with people he doesn't know,' I said.

I heard a voice behind me. 'Well here he is at last. What a handsome creature! Show them in, Aldcroft,' he said to the footman. 'These tars can tell me all about him.' It was Lord Montague himself, returning from an afternoon stroll. He had spotted that we were sailors before he had even set eyes on our faces.

We entered the grand hall and were told to sit with Sydney on a plush red sofa close to the foot of a great winding staircase. I undid his tether and had him perch on my arm. Lady Montague was summoned and came at once to admire their new pet.

Lord Montague was cordial, considering our different stations in life. 'Had a letter from Governor King over the summer, telling me to expect a delivery. Were you in charge of the bird during the voyage?

'Capital, capital,' he said, rubbing his hands together. 'Tell me all about him. What does he eat? What does he like to do? Can he talk? I've heard these birds are marvellous conversationalists.'

I started to tell him, and the more I talked, the sadder I felt. I hadn't realised how fond I had become of Sydney.

'You have to be very careful with him, especially to begin with,' I concluded. 'He's shy with strangers, but he's affectionate with people who treat him well.'

As I talked, I stroked the top of Sydney's head. Lord Montague leaned over to him and said, 'So, I'll bet you're missing the sunshine in New South Wales?'

'He doesn't actually *make* conversation, sir,' I said cheekily. I was feeling light-hearted and this was certainly one occasion when I could make fun of a toff and not face a flogging.

Montague's manner changed in an instant. 'I'm not an imbecile, lad.' Then he softened. He sat next to me on the sofa and beckoned me to hand over the bird. Sydney hopped obligingly from my arm to his.

He put out a hand to stroke Sydney's head. 'Don't peck him, please don't peck him,' I thought.

Emboldened, Montague leaned closer and cooed, 'You are a pretty bird.' At once the cockatoo nipped him on the nose and soiled his trousers. Montague yelled and recoiled in disgust, frightening Sydney even more. He flew up the grand staircase and settled on the topmost banister.

It was time to leave. As we were shooed out of the door, I heard Montague say to his wife, 'I wonder what that thing tastes like? Chicken, d'you think? Or maybe pheasant?'

'Don't you dare,' was the last I heard of that conversation. I hoped Sydney didn't start chirping out his old war cry 'Show us yer arse', at least not until the family had got to know him better.

We spent the rest of the day looking at notices in shop windows for lodgings and found a room in a boarding house close to Covent Garden and the Strand. It was small and expensive, being so close to the middle of things, but clean enough. 'It'll do for a couple of days,' Richard said.

When we'd settled in we wrote our letters. I told my mother and father I had returned safely to England, where I was living, and that I would visit Norfolk soon, but I didn't say when. I loved my family but our village of Wroxham offered the greatest reason for a boy to go to sea. Life there revolved with the same steady and predictable course as the sails of the windmills that stood around the town.

Rosie was close to there too, on the coast at

Yarmouth, Rosie, my childhood sweetheart, who I had told to forget about me when I was transported to New South Wales. Thinking of Rosie made me sad. Having been so attracted to Bel, I knew Rosie was no longer the girl for me. But I still wondered how our life would have worked out together. Me running a village store, and teaching in the local school, she raising our children.

I wrote to Robert Neville too and received a reply by return of post.

Hon. Robert Neville
12 Grosvenor Square
Mayfair

17th November, 1803

Dear Sam and Richard,

How fortunate that your letter should reach me while I am staying in London on leave. I am delighted to hear you are both safe and well. I cannot tell you how pleased I was to hear about your pardon. We must meet at the earliest opportunity. Will you both come for dinner tonight at the family home? My father and mother are both anxious to make your acquaintance.

Would five o'clock be acceptable?

Your true friend

Robert

The idea of meeting Robert's family filled me with trepidation. They were very grand. And what would we wear? We had our sailor's slops and they were looking threadbare after a trip across the world. 'We need to go shopping,' said Richard. 'Fine clothes ahoy.'

A tailor would take a week to make new clothes. We would just have to go dressed as we were and hope the family would understand. Although we cleaned ourselves up and put on fresh clothes I still felt shabby as we set out for the Nevilles' London home.

Robert greeted us with a gleeful hug. We had not seen him for over two years and he had grown taller and stouter. He seemed every inch the young gentleman. The boy I had first known on the *Miranda* had gone. 'You both need some meat on your bones,' he said to Richard and me. 'Good thing we've quite a banquet before us.'

We were ushered into a hall even grander than Lord Montague's. The Nevilles' house was lit by myriad candles, their light twinkling in chandeliers, casting a warm glow over the plush furniture and rich oil paintings of country landscapes and horses. There were also portraits of several generations of the Neville family. I assumed they were anyway; they all had the same look about them.

As I gazed around at this extraordinary splendour, I was introduced to Robert's family. There were two younger brothers, Charles and Henry, one already a midshipman by the look of him, the other only nine or ten and dressed in a smart slate-grey jacket. Lady Neville was a vision of floating silk and lace. She offered us both her hand to kiss and whispered, 'Thank you for saving my son's life.'

Finally, there was Viscount Neville himself. He too was in grey silk with a bright red embroidered waistcoat. He was every bit as distinguished as the governors and admirals I had come across over the previous few years. He exuded power and authority and I could imagine him being a terrifying man to work under. But to us, he was charm and affability.

We dined on goose, served with several bottles of fine wine. 'Shame we've fallen out with those Frenchies,' said the Viscount. 'My cellar's running low on wine and I'd love to sail over there to replenish it.'

Such food, after months of leathery salt pork and dried peas, tasted unreal. We had enjoyed our pub meals since coming ashore but I had quite forgotten how mouth-wateringly delicious well-cooked food could be. The goose was rich and pungent, and I had to stop myself gobbling it down like a starving dog. I didn't want Robert's family to think his friend was some sort of wild urchin.

Richard and I were made to tell the whole story of our near hanging, transportation, and time in New South Wales. We skipped the bit about felling a tree on Lewis Tuck's cottage.

Some time towards the end of the evening, Viscount Neville fixed me with a stern eye and said, 'And what of your future, Sam? Do you intend to return to the sea?'

'I do, sir,' I said confidently. 'But not yet. I went to sea to find adventure, and I've had sufficient to last me a lifetime. For now, I'd like to spend a month or two on land. I want to enjoy some fresh food and days that aren't marked out by the ship's bell.'

'And would you enlist in the Royal Navy or do you intend to sail a merchantman?'

This was a tricky question. I decided honesty was the best policy.

'I started with the merchant fleet, sir, and I expect this offers me the best chance of advancement. I can only hope to sail before the mast in the Royal Navy. On a merchant ship I can pick and choose my Captain and companions, and the length of voyage. On a Navy ship I cannot.'

Viscount Neville nodded sagely. 'You have a wise head on your shoulders, Sam. But you will do well in the Navy. I am prepared to help you become a midshipman, if you would like that. I would be pleased to see you serving alongside Robert again.'

I was flabbergasted, and I replied with care. 'Thank you, sir. It would be an honour to serve alongside Robert. But I need to think about this. For now, I hardly even know what I'll be doing tomorrow morning.'

He nodded and turned to Richard. 'That goes for you too, young fellow, although I would surmise that you intend to return to Massachusetts?'

Richard looked astonished and for a second I saw a gleam of mischief in his eye. His face seemed to be saying 'You must be joking!' For one horrible moment, I thought he was going to launch into a wine-fuelled rant about the Royal Navy being full of high-born snobs and being heartily sick of them and their stuck-up manner.

I kicked him under the table. The gleam faded. To my great relief he said instead, 'I'm grateful for your offer, sir. But I'm set on returning to the United States.'

'How extraordinary,' I thought, 'to have such an opportunity.' Already I was beginning to doubt the wisdom of my response. I knew in my heart I'd be foolish not to take up Neville's offer. A country boy like me could never afford the schooling, the uniform, nor the equipment necessary to become a midshipman. And even more crucially, people like me, or more to the point my father, did not have the influence to secure such an appointment. I hoped I had not destroyed my chance by not seizing the opportunity as soon as it was offered.

It was after midnight when we prepared to leave. As we stood in the hall, Viscount Neville called Robert into a room to talk to him privately. Then they both came out to see us off.

'My coach and four will take you home,' said the Viscount. 'You never know quite who you'll meet out on the street, and you boys are rather close to the rookeries of St Giles and Holborn.'

Robert said, 'You know, we have a small property to rent close to St James's Park. You can stay for three shillings a month between you. Father suggested it just now. No sense running up a big bill where you are. You could move in as soon as you like.'

'What good fortune!' I said to Richard, as our coach trundled over cobbled streets back to Covent Garden. 'We can stay here for longer on such a low rent!'

We were both flying! 'Hurrah!' we said and burst out laughing. 'You know you'd be mad not to take up that offer of a midshipman's post?' Richard said.

'I do know,' I said. 'But the thought of another endless posting, especially the North Sea in winter, and all that burgoo and scotch coffee, and maggoty meat, and sleeping in the stinking hold alongside hundreds of other seamen, the cat o' nine tails, bullying bosun's mates, cannon balls screeching over to take the limbs from my body . . . it's all too horrible.'

Richard said, 'But you'll be an officer, you'll receive better food, better quarters, and the bosun's mates would be doing what you told them rather than hitting you with a rope! And if you pass your exams and become a lieutenant, what next? You could grow rich on prize money from captured warships *and* see the world.'

His face lit up. 'On the other hand, you could always come to Boston. Plenty of opportunity there for a lad like you. Think about it, Sam. Even if you take up old man Neville's offer to train as a midshipman, you'll still have to go to sea in a man-o'-war and everything that goes with it. Come to Boston, and you'll work as a junior officer on a merchant ship. You'll be a captain one day. I hope to be. No chance of that in the British Navy.'

That was a tempting idea too. But I was not ready to leave England, or give up sailing English vessels. I did not like the idea of being a foreigner to my fellows on ship, and leaving England would feel like a betrayal, especially with us still at war with France.

Viscount Neville's offer dangled in front of me like forbidden fruit. I had meant it when I said I was not ready to return to sea. The dark side of the Navy was still too fresh in my mind. But the money we had made on the *Orion* would be spent soon enough and I would have to make a living. I wondered what else I could do. London was a city of endless opportunities – I could

CHAPTER 11

London Life

We moved to our new lodgings in Marlborough Road the next day. It was only a few minutes from St James's Park. It wasn't long before I started to get a feel for London, and the place was every bit as exciting as I hoped it would be. Robert visited frequently to take us on trips to the British Museum or public science lectures at the Royal Institution.

But like the Navy, London had its dark side. Right outside our front door were beggar women with babies in their arms, and girls younger than us offering their bodies for money. There were pickpockets and thieves too and Robert cautioned us never to leave a window open in the house, lest we be broken into. 'The burglars work with young children. They slip them through an open window and the child opens the front door.'

Strolling through St James's Park, a young lad walked straight into me. 'Beggin' your pardon, sir,' he said and hurried off. Richard was behind me and saw the boy whip a hand into my coat and take my purse. The two of us hared down the road after him. But when we turned into the back alley we'd seen him dive down, he was there with three other boys, their knives glinting in the dull light. We ran back to the high street as fast as our legs would carry us.

'We could have had them, Sam,' said Richard, who felt a little bashful about running away. 'They were just urchins.'

'Don't be daft,' I said to him. 'We're not in the Navy any more. Would you want to kill a boy for a few pennies, or risk your own life for the cost of a meal and a few pints of ale?'

What sickened me most were the public hangings. They were always well attended. One day, the three of us went to St Paul's Cathedral. Robert's uncle was the Dean there and we were allowed to climb to the top to admire the view. On our way home we walked into a large crowd close to Newgate Prison. 'Is this some sort of fair?' wondered Robert.

'Naaah, there's a hangin',' said a chestnut-seller.

The crowd was dangerously excited. As they waited, a man with a small monkey running up and down his arm offered extraordinary cures for their ailments. 'MAGNETIC TRACTORS TO PULL OUT DIS-EASE,' he shouted into a voice trumpet, 'SPIRIT OF PEARL FOR MADNESS AND DROPSY.' People flocked to hand over their money.

There were children there too – awaiting the spectacle with the same ghoulish glee as their parents. Having almost been the victim of the hangman myself, and seen several executions in the Navy, I knew first hand the ter-ror and anguish behind this display of official justice. Or so I thought.

Ordinarily, none of us would have stayed to watch, but as we walked away the hangman's victim was ush-ered through the prison gates to the scaffold in front of the square. I looked on him with pity, but as he appeared the crowd gave a massive cheer. Curiosity made us turn back. I wondered if the crowd would surge forward and rescue him, but a phalanx of soldiers, five deep with muskets and bayonets, surrounded the scaffold.

The man was wearing his finest clothes. He looked like a wedding guest and sauntered up the steps of the scaffold without a care in the world. Raising his hands for silence, he began to speak in a clear, confident voice.

'My old ma always told me I'd die with my boots on.' The crowd laughed and whistled its support. 'But I've had plenty of fallings out with the old witch and I've always delighted in proving her wrong.' He kicked his boots off and threw them into the crowd. There was a frantic struggle to claim them.

Speech over, he waved and removed his hat, so the hangman could slip the noose around his neck.

'He's got enough pluck for ten men,' said Robert.

The deed was quickly accomplished as his friends tugged at his feet to hasten the work of the rope.

Richard understood what that performance was all about. 'It's his way of cocking a snook at the authorities,' he said. 'He's supposed to be terrified. But if he can show them he doesn't give a fig then he's won. The crowd came here to cheer him on. They want to raise two fingers to the establishment too.'

The longer we stayed in London, the safer we felt. We'd been in combat and knew we could handle ourselves in a fight. As the weeks went by, Richard and I became careless about the areas we visited. Although we never said as much, we would dare each other to see who would be first to back out of a dangerously seamy riverside pub.

One Tuesday afternoon we were in the North Star close by Southwark dockside. Most of the dinnertime trade had come and gone. Now there were just a few stragglers – the roughest-looking men in the pub. They looked so villainous and seedy among the dingy furnishings I thought Mr Hogarth would have loved to sketch them as subjects for one of his engravings.

Two of them, on the far side of the room, were engaged in an endless game of vingt-et-un. One had several fingers missing, the other an eyepatch. Each swore like a trooper (which they probably used to be) when they lost to the other, slamming down his cards in a fit of temper. I kept expecting the landlord to come over and stop them gambling in his pub, but instead, when trade died down, he went to join them.

To our right were another couple of brutes. They started off talking in whispers but the more they drank the louder they became. One had recently been released from Newgate Prison. 'It's better than the workhouse, I tells yah. If you got money, you can get anything y'like. Brandy, couple o' doxies, even the keys to the front door.'

When they ran out of conversation they started playing dice. Looking round at us, one of them said, 'You look like useful sorts. You boys is sailors, aincha? Come an' join us. See if y'can beat us.'

Neither Richard or I had ever gambled in our lives. I was about to make an excuse when Richard said, 'Just need a leak, mate, then we'll be with you.'

We both went to the urinal on the other side of the building.

'Is this a good idea?' I said. We were both a bit drunk, and I was feeling rattled.

Richard sniggered. 'They look like a right couple of villains. Let's just sit with them for a bit and see what they've got to say for themselves.'

They introduced themselves as John and William and bought us a couple of pints of ale. We began to play a dice game called hazard, where you have to guess the number to be thrown. We had seen enough sailors play to know the rules. John placed a farthing on the table, and I matched it with an identical stake. Drunk though I was, I noticed how low his bid was and immediately began to feel better. This didn't feel like a swindle and sure enough, we kept playing for similarly low wagers, money crossing to and fro in almost equal amounts.

They weren't out to cheat us, they were sizing us up. We carried on buying each other drinks and listened to them boast about their adventures with the 'night plunderers', as the warehouse robbers called themselves. We carried on drinking, playing along with them, fascinated to discover what they were up to.

'You boys lookin' to earn a couple o' bob?' said William. 'There's a merchantman just come in from the West Indies. Hogsheads of tobacco and sugar. There for the takin'.'

We wobbled our heads side to side, trying to appear noncommittal.

I started to feel uneasy when some of their friends joined us. One told us he made a packet as a body-snatcher, supplying fresh corpses for medical students to dissect. 'You boys game?' he said. 'There's ten shilling in it for you. I know plenty at the hospitals who'll take 'em. Got your own spade? There's two fresh graves at St Anne's, Limehouse. We'll have to go tonight, mind, before someone else nabs 'em.'

We kept turning down their offers of 'work' and they began to get suspicious. 'You aint noses are you?' said John.

It was time to go. I should have been more fright-ened but I was now so drunk this all felt like it was happening to someone else. They followed us out into the street and we were dragged into an alley. 'This is it,' I thought, 'we're going to get murdered.' I expected to see the flash of a knife, but we weren't worth killing. A punch to the stomach winded me and as I doubled over I could feel my pockets being fleeced. Then they were gone. We both lost a few shillings. I thought we got off lightly.

This was Richard's cue to leave. Next morning, as we nursed our hangovers, he announced, 'Fun's over. Time to go before something nastier happens!' I supposed it was time for me to visit my parents in Norfolk too.

Richard's departure was swift. Almost at once he was taken on to a returning American merchantman. On the night before the ship sailed, we dined with Robert at his club. 'You must visit Boston, the both of you!' said Richard. 'I have no doubt we will see each other again.'

I was sure of it too, otherwise I would have been dejected to see him go. Richard had been my greatest friend. He was like a brother. After we bade farewell to Robert he said, 'You'd have a brilliant future in Massachusetts. My father would find you work. You'd soon make your fortune.'

We talked long into the night. The next day he walked up the gangplank and shouted, 'See you in Boston!' Then he was gone.

In their letters my mother and father were increasingly indignant that I had not yet visited them. I had been in London three months now, so they did have a point.

It was a slow and tedious journey back to Norfolk. The countryside of England was winter weary. My companions in the coach were a corpulent merchant, his mean little wife and their sour-faced daughter. 'Not long till spring,' I said with a smile. But my attempts at starting a conversation were haughtily rebuffed.

I had written ahead, and when I reached the coaching inn in Norwich my father was there with my brother Tom, waiting with the horse and cart. I'm embarrassed to admit there were tears when we met.

CHAPTER 12

Back from the Dead

My father looked in rude health and Tom seemed to have grown up. He was still shy but had developed a certain steeliness – no doubt after one too many farmers had sold him rotten vegetables.

Home was exactly as I remembered it. My mother stood waiting by the door and ran up the garden path to embrace me. Enfolded in her arms I felt as if I were nine years old, giving her a hug as I came home from school. It was good to feel that safe again.

'Let me look at you,' she said, tears running down her

cheeks. 'Last time we met . . . I thought we'd never see you again. It's like you've come back from the dead.' For an instant I was transported back to the deck of the prison hulk at Portsmouth and remembered the precious ring she'd given me then. I still carried it round my neck and returned it with a proud flourish.

I ran around the house, looking in every room, vaulting up the stairs three at a time, to remind myself of life before I went to sea. The smell of the place – the earthy whiff of vegetables in the shop at the front of the house, my mother's cooking, the furniture polish, and the roaring fire, all took me back to boyhood.

It had been nearly four years since I last stood in this house. So much had changed in my life, yet everything here remained the same. Even the china figurines of the young lady with her ball gown and parasol and the young buck with his musket and hunting dog were in exactly the same spot.

'What took you so long to come back and see us, Sam?' my mother asked after the initial flurry of our greeting.

'Harriet, don't chide the boy as soon as he's home,' said my father.

I heard a clucking out in the yard and rushed out to see the chickens. 'William got had by a fox,' said my father. Mary and Matilda scurried away from me. I was a stranger now.

We ate a succulent beef joint, with thick onion gravy and potatoes and cabbage. My father opened a bottle of wine too – a French claret that must have cost him half a week's takings. 'Well you've certainly learned how to drink,' he said with some disapproval, as I guzzled it down. 'Better make that last, Sam. There's no more in the house.'

That evening we sat around the fire, and I talked long into the night. There was so much to tell them. Tom grew bored. He wasn't interested in New South Wales, or Sumatra, or even London.

'There's nothing there that would tempt *me* away from Norfolk,' he said with a weary sigh and went up to bed.

After he'd gone my father said, 'Funny how two boys can be so different.'

'Thank heaven,' said my mother. 'I couldn't bear to have both my lads away from me all the time. How long you staying for, Sam?'

'I'd like to see in the spring, maybe even the summer, if there's enough for me to do,' I said. 'That is, if you won't mind having me in the house?'

'Stay as long as you like, Sam,' said my father with a big smile. 'You know we want you to stay here in Norfolk. I'm sure a lad like you will find profitable employment.'

I didn't want to talk about what I might be doing in

the future. I didn't even know myself. So I finally asked the question I had been dying to raise all evening. 'And how are the Hookes? Any news of Rosie.'

They exchanged uneasy glances. 'She cried for months when you were transported,' said my mother. 'Mrs Hooke told me she got terribly thin. And there wasn't much of her in the first place. We haven't seen her for a couple of years. But six months ago Mr Hooke came by. Tells us she's doing well. She has a job as a nursery governess for a local family. Very grand they are. One of their footmen's taken a shine to her. I hear she's engaged to be wed. Mr Hooke says he's a good lad. Got prospects. He'll make a butler by the time he's thirty.'

I smiled but felt a stab of regret. I still had a tender spot for Rosie. Had I been right to tell her to forget about me when I left for New South Wales? I had honestly believed I would never be coming back.

The next morning I took a long walk around the fields surrounding the village. It was a bright winter's day and the sunshine had a warmth I had not felt for months. The trees were still bare, but a few daffodils had appeared. I was conscious of being truly alone for the first time in years. Apart from the cows, staring at me in their curious way, there was not another living thing in sight. It was a delicious feeling. After years spent crowded in a ship with scores or hundreds of other people, such solitude felt luxurious. I thought of the sour stench of the cleansing vinegar and sulphur on the *Orion* as we lolled adrift in the doldrums, trying to slake our thirst on warm sour water. The pump in our backyard provided the sweetest water I had ever tasted.

Whether I would remain in Norfolk or not, I did not know. For now, my parents were happy for me to stay, helping out in the shop and the school. I was enjoying the simple pleasures of being with my family again, and living without fear of death or dreadful punishment.

In the shop I noticed how well Tom dealt with his customers. 'Got those peas in you wanted, Mrs Polgrave.' 'And how's little Emma, Mrs Gage? Here's a barley sugar to put a smile back on her face!' He knew them all by name, and their children. The shop was doing well. I was pleased for him. We never had much in common, but Tom had obviously found his vocation.

The schoolhouse was exactly the same, save for all those new faces. I enjoyed helping my father with another generation of Williams and Toms and Elizabeths and Marys. Seeing my father at work filled me with admiration for him and reminded me where I had gained my avid curiosity. He was strict – that was a matter of self-preservation – but he was quite genuine in his determination to teach his charges.

The school room was as bright and full of interesting objects as its tiny parish fund allowed. There was a nature table with fir cones and shells and animal skulls, maps of Great Britain and the world on the wall and embroidered samplers in glass frames. Every morning he would chalk a curious riddle on his blackboard, which the children had to copy and then work out for themselves.

In wars and in battle I have ever been
Yet where there is fighting I never am seen
Nor do I in tumult or riots appear
But if there's a rabble I'm sure to be there.

It was disappointing to discover the answer to such a curious conundrum was merely the letter A.

Our village parson, the Reverend Chatham, had donated books and instructive toys now his own children had grown up. There were puzzles, paper dolls, table games – all battered and faded, but still quite usable – and all far too expensive for the village children to own themselves. These items were almost sacred to my father – he was a strong believer in learning through play, a fanciful modern notion to some of the parents who believed only the birch could instil the rudiments of the alphabet in their children. When Italy went missing from the jigsaw of Europe, there was a grand inquisition. Nobody confessed but the piece turned up the next day.

I was asked to tell the children which countries I'd visited and they listened spellbound as I stood before the map of the world. I told them of the Barbary apes of Gibraltar, the kangaroos of New South Wales and the tigers of Sumatra. I liked to think I planted a seed in the minds of some of the boys, and they too would one day go to sea to find adventure. I spoke too, as gently as I could, about the hardship and cruelty of life in the Navy. I was determined they should be told the full story. I felt quite elated when I'd finished. 'You're a natural, Sam,' said my father.

By the early summer I was beginning to feel restless. The village pub, with its earth floor and its reticent labourers, was a dreary place where nothing exciting was ever going to happen. Here in Wroxham every day was the same. At sea a hundred things could happen that were different from the day before.

The gentle pleasures of teaching were beginning to wane. I knew it was a valuable job – few people could do more for their fellows than a good teacher – but I couldn't bear the thought of watching each batch of children go out into the world while I stayed there, season after season, year after year.

My parents took such an obvious pleasure in having

me home, I did not like to think about leaving them, so I hid my restlessness and made the most of our time together. But the familiar yearning to get away that had first taken me to sea when I was thirteen had returned with a vengeance.

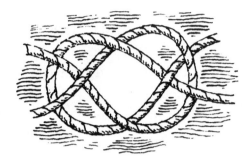

CHAPTER 13

Adrift

I decided to see the summer through in Wroxham. Then I would return to London, and work as a merchant seaman. I could sail from Yarmouth, as I had before, but London offered the greatest opportunities and I missed the excitement of the city. I dreaded telling my parents, but they understood. 'We're surprised you stayed this long,' said my father.

'You never did seem settled,' said my mother sadly.

The money I had made on the *Orion* was nearly gone, and it was time to start earning a proper living again. My father gave me a little to see me on my way 'for helping out in the shop and school'. I felt guilty taking it but it paid for my return to London, and left me with a few weeks' rent for lodgings.

I didn't go back to the Nevilles' house in Marlborough Road. Robert would have returned to sea and I did not want to have his father pressing me to rejoin the Navy. I could not bring myself to make such a fateful decision. I often dreamed of being on a man-o'-war – sometimes coming aboard a new ship, full of trepidation as the crew turned to look at me. But usually my dreams were of combat, of the awful apprehension before the guns started to fire, or being helpless and injured on an abandoned ship, or surrounded by flashing swords and axes in the terrifying whirl of hand-to-hand combat.

I took lodgings near to London Bridge, on the south side. I earned my keep making short trips on merchant ships, a fortnight here to Bristol, a week there to Newcastle.

One autumn morning, during a short stay between voyages, I strolled around a corner into Bermondsey market. Not five yards in front of me was Bel Sparke, picking apples and cherries from a barrow. She was clothed in a plain white dress with a small black belt tied tight around her waist, and a black crocheted shawl around her shoulders to keep out the chill Thames wind. She wore little black boots and a red ribbon to hold the hair away from her face.

I had thought of her often since we'd parted and for a few moments I couldn't keep my eyes off her. Then I thought to hide in the crowd. It would be awkward to talk to her. But too late! She turned and saw me.

Her face lit up, and she rushed over. 'Hello Samuel Witchall, how's that cockatoo of yours?'

Something in me melted. Perhaps I could forgive her a little bit.

'Hello Bel, how's life treating you?'

'Not bad. Back home with my mother and father. They were surprised to see me. I'm keepin' busy. I'm workin' in a milliner's shop. Managed to avoid the fish-gutting after all. Half-day closing today, got the afternoon all to myself! And you?'

We ambled through the market together, then on to the quayside, chatting as we walked. I was pleased to find her in good spirits. 'Do you ever look at the boats and wish you were sailing off somewhere exciting?' I asked.

She nodded. 'Life's been slow since Miss Lizzie died. Her family sent me a few guineas to tide me over while I set about finding work. Her sister said Lizzie had always spoken well of me, and that they would be happy to recommend me to a family if a position became available. I'd like to go back to being a lady's maid – maybe do some more travelling, and meet all kinds of different people.'

'But Bel, you can't count on finding someone else like Lizzie,' I said. 'What would happen if you found yourself sailing off to America or India with someone who treated you like a dog?'

'I've got a good nose for people, me,' she said.

'Are you hungry?' I asked, wanting to talk to her for longer. There were several taverns right by the riverside. 'You know it round here, which is the best?'

Sitting in a smoky room at the Green Man, on rough wooden benches as the sun streamed in through stained-glass windows, I started to feel more at ease.

'Let me buy you a nice hot pie,' she said, and went to the counter. But the tavern had been busy and had sold out of food. 'Come back home, and I'll make something to eat,' she said. 'I only live five minutes away.'

The Sparkes lived in a tall, narrow house close to the quayside, in a street called Cherry Lane. Like the other houses around it, it was wood and plaster rather than brick and although it was the middle of the day it was very dark inside. But it was clean, and the sparse furniture was well cared for.

There was no one at home. 'They're both out workin',' said Bel, 'won't be back 'til later.' I was quite relieved. Mr and Mrs Sparke had often featured in Bel's conversation and not always in a flattering light.

'You sit down and I'll find some food,' she said.

Bel returned with bread and cheese and a couple of the

apples she had just bought. 'After all them months on a ship, I still marvel at the taste of fresh food,' she said.

We talked long into the afternoon and all over again I fell under her spell. She had been lucky with the small-pox. Her scars had healed and took little away from her beauty. She laughed at all my jokes, and she clearly remembered little incidents on the ship between us. I began to realise I must have meant something to her after all.

As the light faded in the late afternoon, she cleared the table and said she would fetch some candles. I went over to the window to stare at the passers-by out on the busy street.

'You best be going, Sam,' she said. 'My dad will be home soon, and he's bound to think the worst of this!'

We agreed to meet again when I was next ashore. It was a promising start.

There was much work in the Merchant Navy for a sailor with a good reputation. After a week or two at sea I could come back and spend a few days in London. I saw Bel whenever I could. She was always happy to meet me, though she told me straight out that her parents disap-proved of our friendship. '"Sailors, they have a wife in every port," that's what my ma says,' Bel said to me with a giggle. '"Don't wanna get mixed up with them."

'I told them you're an old mate from my trip around

the world and there's no funny business goin' on.' She looked me straight in the eye when she said that. 'Seemed to calm them down a bit.'

I would also regularly take the stagecoach to Norwich and my father would come and meet me with his horse and cart and we'd clip-clop back to Wroxham for a few days. Now and then I would catch up with Robert Neville when he was on leave in London. It was always a pleasure to see him, and I enjoyed hearing about life in the Royal Navy. Exciting thought it was, I didn't miss it. He said no more about his father's offer.

In the spring of 1805, soon after I turned eighteen, I came across a crippled merchant seaman begging in the streets close to my home. Something about the man provoked my pity and I took him to a local tavern and bought him food and ale. We talked all afternoon, and he told me of his fate – one that was shared by far too many merchant seamen. Unlike Royal Navy sailors, he explained, he could not depend on Greenwich Hospital for charity now that he had become too ill to make a living. He had to beg to keep himself alive.

For several days this preyed on my mind. It was, after all, one possible future if I stayed in the merchant service. I discussed it with Bel. 'Maybe you need to get away from the sea, Sam,' she said. 'Try and get a job on the harbour-side. Maybe at the East India Docks? Maybe you could find work at Chatham, with the shipbuilders or ropemakers? Your experience at sea must be useful somewhere?'

But none of these appealed to me. I thought hard about going to Boston, to find Richard. But I knew Bel wouldn't come with me and I didn't want to leave her behind. I could not go on living in this aimless fashion, working on and off as it suited me. I had to do something more with my life, and what I really wanted, still, was adventure.

CHAPTER 14

My Friend the Rat

In the summer of 1805 I came back from a voyage to
Newcastle to find a letter from Robert Neville. Its
content left me feeling uneasy.

Hon. Robert Neville
HMS Intrepid
Cape Finesterre

20th June, 1805

Dear Sam,

I hope this letter finds you well. It's been a good while since we last saw each other, and I'm hoping to be home for a few weeks' leave again in the middle of July. We must meet for a glass of wine.

No doubt you have heard reports that Napoleon has amassed some 200,000 soldiers at Boulogne, from where, I'm sure you know, you can see the cliffs at Dover. This 'Armée d'Angleterre', as it is known, is set to invade us. Should the Royal Navy fail to prevent their crossing the Channel I think it's fair to say the country would fall in a matter of weeks. We both know our own army is no match for the French.

In this atmosphere of national crisis I fear greatly that the press gangs will be descending mob-handed on the ports of England to muster every available tar to man our warships. You are bound to become a victim of their activities.

Perhaps you could think again about joining the Navy? We need good men like you. Our liberty is threatened! Do consider what I'm asking and let me know. Write to Grosvenor Square and I hope to see you shortly.

Your true friend

Robert

He hadn't mentioned his father's offer about training to become a midshipman. Was that still on the table? The letter stirred up other feelings too. I still did not want to go back to the Navy, but I felt guilty about it now rather than defiant. My country was in peril.

The press gangs had been lying low since I returned to the sea. Now they were sure to be busy. Although I knew this to be certain, I had heard from other merchant seamen that they were concentrating their activities on the Navy ports of Plymouth and Portsmouth, and along the south coast.

So why didn't I write back at once saying I would join up with him? I intended to, but three days hence I was to sail to Edinburgh with Thomas Findlay, a captain who was reputed to pay handsomely and treat his men well. I'd heard he was looking for a third mate for his ship and I wanted to impress him. And when I came back Bel had promised to meet me. I had not seen her for several weeks and had missed her keenly. I resolved to contact Robert when I returned. I would put off my decision until then.

The trip went well, aside from some delay on the return leg due to unfavourable headwinds. The Captain was as good as his reputation and when we returned to London he announced he would be sailing again shortly, this time to Whitby, and would take on crew at the Bridge House Inn, Bermondsey, on the afternoon of 15th July. His final words to me were, 'You know your trade well,

Witchall. I could use a man like you as a regular part of my crew.'

This was promising. That 15th July morning I walked from London Bridge to Bermondsey, intending to get there in good time to have lunch before the Captain arrived. At the inn I fell into conversation with some other sailors I'd met on the Edinburgh trip. They grumbled about the press gangs getting closer to home – Chatham and Sheerness, even Woolwich. 'I hear Findlay's looking for a third mate,' said one of my companions. 'That makes you a ship's officer. Press gangs can't touch merchant officers.' I listened with great interest.

The inn was filling up with sailors. Findlay's reputation was obviously widely known. He arrived soon after one o'clock but his hopes of recruiting a crew were quickly dashed. Before he called us to order, five burly thugs appeared at the front entrance. Behind them, through the open door, I caught a glimpse of a red tunic. There were some marines with them too. We all knew instinctively that the press gang had arrived and there was a rush for the back door. They were waiting there too, five of them in their scruffy civilian rags, and another squad of marines, muskets at the ready, bayonets attached. We scattered like a shoal of minnows before the jaws of a pike, running every way, wherever a gap presented itself.

I narrowly avoided the grasp of one of them, but before I'd gone another step, another grabbed my scarf. It was a beautiful cream Indian cotton one, with an embroidered pattern along the edge. Bel had given it to me for my eighteenth birthday. It ripped in his grubby hand and then slipped off my neck. He grabbed my arm, and out of anger and desperation I aimed a punch at his head. He went down with a sulphurous oath and I saw my chance. A narrow alley behind a riverfront warehouse lay unguarded before me. Not daring to look round I sprinted with all the strength my legs could muster. I ran the whole length of that alley then stopped to walk out on to the high street at the end of it. I peered round to see if anyone was pursuing me. They were busy elsewhere.

I set off back to my lodgings along the southern embankment of the Thames, waiting for my breathing to steady. By the time I reached London Bridge I was beginning to feel tired and disappointed. How would I make contact with Captain Findlay again? Turning into Tooley Street, right there by the Prince William pub, I saw a mob of ten or so men dragging a couple of tars off. They could only be another press gang. Today the impressment service had descended on London in full force.

They were marching straight towards me. I wondered if I should just walk on and hope they would not realise

I was a sailor. But then I thought they might grab me anyway. Press gangs did not only take men who were obviously seamen. Being young and healthy was sometimes quite enough.

I began to walk quickly in the other direction. Then I heard shouting. 'Hey, you, Jack Tar!' I turned – four of them were running towards me. I fled again, coming out at the top of Tooley Street, just before London Bridge. I could try to outrun them across the bridge, which was crowded with people, carriages and wagons, or I could hide beneath it.

I ran down the stone steps to the embankment and on to the tidal mud and shingle. Through the stone arches I could see what was clearly a pressing tender. Men were being ferried aboard from a rowing boat, and marines were waiting for them on the deck. I prayed no one would see me as I dashed beneath the bridge. Above I could hear the clatter of feet and hoped I would make the underside before one of the gang peered over and spotted me.

There among the sewage and weeds and driftwood at the base of the first stone arch was the remains of a hefty barrel – its rotten mouldy wood smashed in around its rusty hoops. I dashed across and pulled it over me, dislodging several pints of fetid mud and water, which soaked through my jacket and shirt before creeping slowly down the back of my trousers. The intact part of the barrel was large enough to cover me if I pulled my legs up. I lay there peeping through a crack between the planks.

The underside of bridges are strange, eerie places. It had been a hot summer's day but here it was clammy and cold, especially with the water seeping through my clothes. There was plenty of other rubble down here too – making my hiding place less obvious. The skeleton of a rotten rowing boat lay close to the water, along with bits of tattered canvas and rope, discarded clothing, and an old hat squashed flat among the pebbles.

Waiting in this almost-silence reminded me of the awful calm before going into action. My heart was beating hard and I noticed everything around me in vivid detail. It was a strangely still spot, here under the bridge, with all the clamour and bustle just above. The river made dancing reflections on the vaulting arch and I could hear the water lapping on the shingle.

I also heard a scurrying just below my line of sight. There, sitting boldly between my chest and the edge of the barrel, was a great fat rat. His whiskers tickled my skin where the shirt buttons strained against my chest. He looked up at me with curious black eyes.

I stroked his fur with a finger. He didn't seem to mind. Rats, they were always the enemy on a ship, to be driven out with sulphur and battered to death. But this one seemed as tame as a house cat. Then I wondered if he was crawling with fleas. I knew these creatures were infamous carriers of disease.

There was a sudden crunch of footsteps close by. It could only be thugs from the press gang. Come to look for me.

I hardy dared breathe. I could hear them talking, their voices echoing around under the bridge. 'You sure he came dahn 'ere?' said one, between great lungfuls of air. He sounded shattered.

'No,' said the other. 'You sure he ran over the bridge?'

'Worth lookin' for tho' ain't 'e? Wouldn't have run away unless he was sure we'd nab 'im.'

The footsteps came closer. 'Tell you wot,' said the one who was fighting for his breath. 'If we catch the bastard, I'm gonna give him a good hidin'. Makin' us run arfter 'im.'

I shrank a little smaller. I could hear them, poking around with their cutlasses. Surely the barrel was the first place they'd look.

'Wot's under 'ere, I wonder,' said one. They wandered over to me. I could see the stockings of one of them right by the crack in the wood. They were playing now. Taunting me, or not taking themselves entirely seriously. 'Come on out, come on out and get your bleedin' head kicked in,' said one in a sing-song voice as he banged his cutlass on the top of the barrel.

I chose this moment to give my rat a shove. He

bolted out and scuttled away. Both of them recoiled. 'Euuurghh, it's only a soddin' rat,' one of them said with disgust.

They wandered back up the stairway to the embankment.

I stayed put until the tender had pulled away. Emerging dripping wet, covered with stinking mud, feeling like a homeless beggar, I made my way back to my lodgings. I filled my tin bath with water from the pump and scrubbed the dirt from my body and clothes. Then, like a flash of lightning, I remembered Robert's letter. Was I too late? I threw on a fresh pair of clothes and ran as fast as my legs would carry me to Grosvenor Square. Please still be here, I kept saying to myself. Please don't have left for another tour of duty.

There were two clear ways my life could go. Sam Witchall, pressed man, slave to the Navy and the whims of fate and bosun's mates. Or Sam Witchall, midshipman, officer in training, companion to the Honourable Robert Neville. Why had it taken me until now to see that this was the choice that life was offering me?

CHAPTER 15

A Proper Gentleman

I banged on the door of the Nevilles' house in Grosvenor Square. A servant answered, a new fellow who did not know me.

'I've come to see Master Neville,' I announced.

We went through a little ceremony where he established who I was. 'Is Robert here?' I could barely contain my anxiety. 'Has he returned to sea?'

The man looked at me as if I were being terribly impertinent. 'I'm afraid, young man, I'm not at liberty to say.

'One moment,' he said, then closed the door. He

seemed to be gone for ever. If Robert had returned to his ship or the Nevilles were out of town, I would have to waste weeks trying to catch them. I would have to go back to sea to earn my keep, and maybe I would be pressed there?

Eventually, the servant returned. He had obviously been making enquiries and his manner was now more compliant. 'Master Neville is away. But he will be back this evening. I shall tell him you called.'

I went north, past the bustle of Oxford Street and into the quiet of Marylebone. The further away I was from the port and the river, the better. I did not even seek out an inn or coffee house. I wanted to find a place where I could survey the comings and goings, and hide myself in good time if a suspicious-looking gang of toughs should appear on the street. I found a quiet little square and waited, watching the early evening shadows grow longer. All the while I wondered how to couch this conversation. Would they begrudge me for not leaping at the chance to join the Navy when Viscount Neville first made his offer last autumn? There were practical considerations too. If the offer was still open, neither my father or myself could afford to pay for my training, let alone my uniform. Again and again I cursed myself for not taking up the Nevilles' offer earlier.

The local church clock struck seven and I walked back to Grosvenor Square. When I arrived, Robert had been tipped off about my coming. 'Don't take off your coat,' he said. 'We're dining at White's, just Father and you and I.'

White's was a short walk away. The club's plushly decorated interior was quite a contrast to my own humble lodgings. I kept thinking about how I would phrase my request. 'I want to join the Navy because I don't want to be nabbed by the press gang,' seemed a bit ungracious. So far, neither of them had mentioned the subject. But the Viscount made it easy for me.

After the first course of pigeon and crayfish he turned to me and said, 'You have heard the news? Napoleon is stirring up trouble, and London fears an invasion. The press gangs will be out in force. I'd wager you'd be exactly the sort they'll be looking for.' Without waiting for a response, he continued, 'I'm sure we'd all agree that the last thing anyone wants is for you to be pressed again, Sam.'

I nodded enthusiastically. He left the idea hanging in the air.

Our meat course arrived – succulent lamb chops. The red wine the Viscount had ordered was the most delicious I had ever tasted.

After we'd eaten and were sat full of food in an amiable haze, Robert said, 'My father has a proposition for you.'

The Viscount smiled. It was an unsettling smile, rather

like that of a predatory fox I had once seen in a children's storybook. 'I do. You don't have to answer me now, but think seriously about what I'm suggesting.'

Robert was smiling too and nodding his head. I knew they were going to ask me about joining the Navy.

'I'd like to suggest, again, that we find you a berth as a midshipman in His Majesty's Navy. Alongside Robert here. Now what d'you think of that?'

'Thank you, sir,' I replied, a huge sense of relief sweeping over me. I answered carefully, feeling for the right words. I knew that the Viscount would be able to find me a suitable post with ease; it was everything else that worried me. 'But my own income, it's not nearly enough for such a post, and my father would never be able to meet the cost . . .'

Viscount Neville waved his hand to dismiss these concerns. 'Sam, I shall be your patron. I shall fund your training, purchase your uniform and oversee your progress.'

He was talking of hundreds of pounds. 'Sir, I'm very grateful for your kindness, but I could not accept. Perhaps you would allow me to repay you over time?'

Neville nodded. The fox-like smile remained. 'Sam, if it wasn't for you, I would not be sitting here dining with my dear son. Now what is that worth? You can't put a price on it. Supporting your training as a midshipman, and, in time, as a lieutenant, will fulfil two extremely worthy purposes. Firstly, it will thank you for saving Robert's life when the *Miranda* was lost. Secondly, I am convinced you will make a first-rate officer, so it will be a useful service to our nation. I'm going to go home now and leave you two to talk. Sleep on it tonight and tell me your answer tomorrow.'

A nod brought the waiter over to our table and Viscount Neville paid for our meal and ordered another bottle of wine for Robert and me.

After he left we talked more freely.

'You'd be a fool to turn this down, Sam. Besides, the Navy needs men like you. Do it for your country as well as for yourself!'

I did not share Robert's patriotic zeal, in fact I did not really know how serious he was being. I liked my country and my King, but found it hard to believe a government that would press boys into the Navy was any better than any other nation in Europe.

'And all humbug aside,' he continued, 'it's a racing certainty you'll be picked up by a press gang.'

I wanted to blub my grateful thanks for being given a second chance, and offer gushing apologies for not having the wit to take it before. But I thought it wisest not to point this out.

'I'd be honoured to take up your father's offer, Robert,' I said calmly. 'I'm very grateful to you and your family.'

He grinned and raised his glass. 'Well that, my good friend, has made my day.' We drank our wine, then walked out into Piccadilly and the hot summer night. London was such an exciting and beautiful city, at least this part of it was. As I climbed aboard a hackney carriage to take me home, Robert said, 'I think the old man likes the idea of us serving together. We shall look out for each other.'

I lay awake that night, mind racing with these possibilities. When Richard left, I couldn't imagine going back to the Navy without him. It was such a brutal place to be. But now I would have Robert as a companion. That appealed to me. Especially as the division of rank between us would be gone.

The pay alone would be five or six times more than I could expect as an ordinary seaman. And lieutenants were also entitled to a generous slice of prize money from any captured ship. And lieutenants became first lieutenants, and first lieutenants became captains. Unlikely, I knew, but fate had been strange enough to me already, during my time at sea. Who knew what might happen?

I spoke about it to Bel when we met the next day at noon to share our dinner. 'Sam, you must do this,' she said. 'Don't think I won't miss you. I will. But you won't ever have another chance like this. I know you,

Sam Witchall. You wouldn't suit a stay-at-home kind of job. You've got the sea in your bones. Besides, you being a midshipman, you'll get to take leave when your ship comes into port and you and me can meet up then. What d'you think?'

That afternoon I went straight back to Grosvenor Square. I was ushered into the Viscount's study and he signalled me to sit down by his desk. 'We need to establish what your skills are, and what you need to learn. Can you go aloft and furl and reef a sail?'

'Yes.'

'Can you bend and unbend a canvas?'

'Yes.'

'Can you set up the ropes for the hoisting of stores?'

'Yes.'

I interrupted this flow of questions. 'Sir, I've served aboard Navy ships and merchantmen since I was thirteen years old. I'm familiar with all aspects of seamanship.'

'Good. Because you will be questioned at great length, and I need to be sure I'm recommending someone who's worthy of it. Now, how about your navigation?'

'Robert taught me to use a sextant and the constellations to calculate a ship's position at sea.'

'That's all very well, but how's your trigonometry? Calculus?'

I looked blank.

'Right. That's something to remedy. You'll have to join the younger middies and have your lessons aboard ship.'

He tossed me over a copy of the King James Bible.

'Pick a page at random and read me a passage.'

I did and began to read from the Gospel According to John.

'*Then said they unto him, Who art thou? That we may give an answer unto them that sent us. What sayest thou of thyself? And he said I am the voice of him that crieth in the wilderness. Make straight the way of the Lord –*'

'Fine,' barked the Viscount, cutting me off mid-flow. 'You're obviously lettered, and a confident reader with it. You read very well, Sam. Ever thought of becoming a parson?'

I met Robert the following day. We had an appointment at a tailor's in Old Burlington Street which specialised in Navy clothes. I was to be fitted for my midshipman's uniform. He said, 'You're not to worry about the cost, Sam. In fact, I don't want to mention money again. My father insists on it. You'll have the best we can get. There'll be snobbery from some of the other middies when you first join, so I want you looking tip-top to save you from any jibes about your apparel.'

I hadn't thought of that. All the midshipmen I had

come across had been boys from wealthy families. They were all well-spoken. Some, like Robert, were even titled. Until now I hadn't considered what my fellow midshipmen would make of me.

'D'you think there'll be a lot of that?' I asked.

'The midshipmen's berth is a rough and ready place, Sam. I often used to envy you and your mess mates on the *Miranda*. You looked after each other. And when a seaman was caught stealing and sent to run the gauntlet, I thought that was odd. Middies steal from each other all the time. There's a lot of horseplay and dirty tricks – downright tomfoolery really. You'll have to get used to that. Some of these lads are straight from boarding school and it's just a continuation of the high jinks they get up to there.

'You'll have to give as good as you get. Don't forget, the rules for midshipmen are different from the rules for men before the mast. You won't get flogged for fighting a fellow middie, and you won't have to run the gauntlet if you steal from him. You'll have to look after yourself with your fists for the first few months, until they realise you're as good as them, if not a damn sight better.

'And if they become unbearable, then we'll have to remind them that Lord Nelson himself came from a very ordinary background.'

I knew a lot about Nelson, but was curious to learn more about his family.

'His father is only a parson. The family are well-connected but hardly have a penny to rub together.'

Robert's reply made me laugh. I said, 'Where I come from, parsons are considered among the best sort of people.'

The conversation was making me uncomfortable. Still, I thought, having to deal with a few snooty boys would be child's play after the brutal attention of bosun's mates.

The tailor's shop had a beautiful carved wood and glass front. When the bell chimed as we pushed at the door, a fawning assistant appeared at once. The smell of the place, with its polished leather shoes and starched and pressed linen shirts, spoke of luxury way beyond my pocket.

'Good day,' said Robert. 'My friend Mr Witchall here will soon be going to sea. We shall require a uniform for a midshipman.'

I was measured and asked to come back in two days.

On my return I brought Bel with me. 'Ma and dad, they're mightily impressed by all this,' she said with a mischievous twinkle. 'Overnight, you've gone from "that sailor" to "Young Samuel". They don't think you're so bad after all.'

Robert met us at the shop. He and Bel had only met once before and had not taken to each other. She thought him aloof and pompous, especially for someone so young. He said nothing to me about her, but he rarely spoke to her and I couldn't help feeling he thought she was beneath his attention.

Out came the new uniform from its boxes, each item wrapped in thin crinkly paper. My transformation began. I went to a curtained booth and stripped to my undergarments. I felt a mixture of pride, curiosity and fear. I was about to change from Sam Witchall, grocer's son, merchant seaman, and no one in particular, to Midshipman Witchall, Royal Navy, officer in waiting. As soon as I donned this uniform I would be treated differently by the world around me. My hands began to tremble. This was it. I was going back to the Navy. The Navy that almost cost me my life on more occasions than I cared to remember. The Navy that treated its men with cold contempt and cruelty. The Navy that kidnapped sailors from the streets and their ships to crew its men-o'-war. And what's more I was joining *them* – the ones responsible for the cruelty and the kidnapping. Was I doing the right thing? Would I become as callous as some of the officers I had served under, or would I be soft on the men and earn their scorn?

I thought then and there to run out of the shop and not stop until I had reached the inn for the Norwich stagecoach. But Robert and Bel were there. Something, perhaps pride, perhaps cowardice, probably a mixture of the two, made me stay.

I pulled on my breeches, made with a buff yellow cloth fabric from China known as nankeen. Then came a finely tailored linen shirt, a nankeen waistcoat and a black silk handkerchief to tie around my neck. As I removed the jacket from its box, I could see it was a beautiful piece of work – a blue tailcoat in heavy cotton, lined with white silk, and adorned with small gold buttons, each embossed with an anchor. I sat down on the chair provided and pulled on my black leather shoes. They were a perfect fit, and I hoped I had stopped growing, for a new pair six months later would be way beyond my means. Finally, there was the hat – three-cornered with a gold loop and cockade.

This uniform felt strange on me – like dressing up for a part in a performance. It reminded me most of all of dressing as a grand gentleman for the village Christmas play when I was a boy. I felt like a fraud, but I was dying to know what I looked like in this magnificent outfit.

Pulling back the curtain, I stepped out. Robert and Bel were standing apart and had not said a word to each other while I was changing. Robert cheered and Bel began to clap, sheer delight on her face. 'Sam, you look like a proper gentleman,' she said and kissed me on the cheek.

Robert smiled broadly. 'Quite the picture, old chap.

You look the part to a T.' I did too.

The assistant fussed around me, checking the fitting, asking me to stretch and bend my arms, enquiring about my shoes.

'Now let's have a look at the dirks, and the rest of it,' said Robert. I selected a brand new dirk to hang at my belt and shuddered at the price of it – several months' work as a boy seaman. 'And we shall need a watch coat,' said Robert, and I tried on several heavy coats. Just the thing for a freezing night watch. Robert ordered more shirts, breeches and stockings and a large sea chest to keep them in.

The purchase that excited me most was my telescope. Robert insisted we visit an optical instrument shop to buy one 'and damn the expense'. We chose a leather-covered silver brass model. 'Got to have your name on it, so no one can steal it,' said Robert. I held it in my hand, with *Samuel Henry Witchall, R.N.* engraved on the draw tube, and felt delighted at my good fortune.

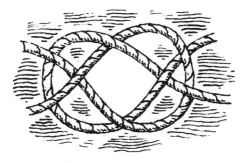

CHAPTER 16

HMS *Victory*

Our posting was decided within days. I was visiting Robert when the despatch arrived. He hurriedly tore it open.

'It's HMS *Victory*, Sam!' He could not have looked more delighted. 'We'll need to catch the Portsmouth coach tomorrow. We're to serve with Lord Nelson again. What a marvellous honour!'

I grinned in amusement at his bulldog enthusiasm. 'Well that will be interesting,' I said, trying to sound a bit excited.

He caught my mood in an instant. 'What's bothering

you, Sam?'

'I've never served on a First Rate,' I said.

'Does it matter?'

I did not know whether I could be totally open with Robert. I owed him so much I did not want to disappoint him. I chose my words with care.

'I'd prefer to take up my first midshipman posting on a Navy ship I know well, like a frigate or a 74.'

'First rates aren't that different from a 74,' said Robert. 'You've got three gun decks rather than two. A hundred or so cannon rather than seventy-four. Eight or nine hundred seamen and marines, rather than five hundred. There'll be a couple of dozen midshipmen too, so you'll not stand out in the way you would on a frigate. Believe me, I felt very conspicuous on the *Miranda*.'

I thought I'd be honest with him. If I couldn't be honest with my closest friend on the ship, I couldn't be honest with anyone.

'Lord Nelson is an extraordinary man,' I said carefully. 'But he's a fearless commander. And sometimes, being fearless is close to being foolhardy.'

I remember well overhearing Lord Nelson on the quarterdeck of the *Elephant*, during the Battle of Copenhagen. He seemed to relish the danger. This set a tremendous example to the men aboard his ship, but when I heard him say 'I would not be elsewhere for thousands' I thought him strange, as any of us on that quarterdeck could have been killed at any second.

Robert wasn't having this. He grasped my arm and spoke fervently. 'Sam – we're weeks, maybe days away from being invaded. D'you want to see Emperor Napoleon on the throne? D'you want to see us all speaking French? D'you want our empire to become the French Imperial Empire? Of course you don't. I can't think of a better man to lead us than Nelson, even if the fellow is a damned philanderer!'

We both laughed at that. Nelson's abandonment of his own wife for Lady Emma Hamilton was common knowledge. I was glad Robert mentioned it. Perhaps he wasn't too starry-eyed about the Admiral.

I took a deep breath. 'When you join the Navy,' I said, 'you have to expect that you might be killed. I also know I'd like to survive this posting! Lord Nelson likes to lead from the front. That's what makes him the hero he is. All of us on the *Victory*, we're going to be right there at the front, bearing the brunt of the battle. That's what serving with Lord Nelson actually means.'

'*Dulce et decorum est, pro patria mori*,' said Robert. He was making me feel stupid again. 'It's Latin. "It is sweet and fitting to die for one's country."'

'Do all the middies speak Latin?' I asked, trying to change the subject. I was anxious about my new comrades-in-arms.

'Most of them, I expect,' said Robert. 'But don't

worry about that. While they were wiling away the time studying Greek and Latin at Eton or Winchester, you were climbing up the mainmast to set the topsails, or fighting the Spanish. That's worth a hundred dead languages in this profession.

'Now, before we go to sea we have an extremely important venture to attend to. We shall call at Fortnum and Mason's to stock up on supplies! Let's see if we can fill these chests to the brim.'

This was another unfamiliar luxury. I had never visited this famous shop, but I knew its reputation as a provider of exotic groceries. Robert had been there many times before, and knew exactly what to get. 'Crystallised peppermints, marmalade fruitcake, anchovy paste, rhubarb and ginger preserve, goose foie gras en gelée, whole baby pears in calvados . . .' The assistant went scurrying off to every corner of the shop to locate these delicacies. 'They'll all keep for months on end,' Robert said to me. We also stocked up on horse-radish sauce, fruit and nut chutney, lemon curd – anything with a bit of a zing to make our salt meat and ship's biscuits more bearable.

I returned to my lodgings to settle my bills and gather my belongings. I was severing the ties of my ordinary life and preparing to go to war. I went to see Bel but she was neither at home or at the milliner's shop. I wrote a hurried note telling her I would let her know when I would be back in London, and prayed that I would see her again.

Left alone with my thoughts, I wondered why I was doing this. I did not believe God was an Englishman, but I felt in my heart that he would want us to vanquish the tyrant Napoleon. Did I want to die for my country? Robert professed he would be willing to. I ardently hoped I could avoid that fate.

More than that, I was concerned about being found wanting by my fellows and the ship's crew. I was told that midshipmen called the ordinary sailors 'the people', but I couldn't bring myself to do that. I wasn't one of them any more. But would I deserve their respect? Would I be worthy of my rank?

When I had fought before, I had been under threat of execution for showing fear before the enemy. Every move had been watched by marines or officers with the power to shoot me dead if I flinched from my duty. I had also been so frantically busy, ferrying gunpowder from the ship's hold to the guns, that I had barely time to think. Now I would be the one in command. I would be the one thinking and ordering and the prospect was much more frightening than running around doing my duty.

As we rattled and jolted on the coach to Portsmouth, I took a special pleasure in looking at the late summer fields, now filling with hay bales as the farm workers gathered in the harvest. I did not know when I would see life on land again, if at all.

At last the spires and mastheads of Portsmouth stood out above the trees and chimney pots. We spent our last night on shore in a tavern and ate a fine pork joint. Next morning we took a supply ship out to the *Victory*. Stepping away from the quayside and on to the bobbing boat, I had a fearful premonition. 'Let's pray that we both set foot on land again!' I said to Robert.

'And let's pray that we both fight bravely and bring honour to our ship and our country!' said Robert. I did find his zealous patriotism a little wearisome. Seeing he expected a response, I raised an imaginary toast: 'Ship and Country!'

That's what Richard would have done. He was a master at playing the game. Being a midshipman meant acting a part. Under intense scrutiny from both the officers and the crew, I would be required to wear my patriotism on my sleeve.

It was 20th August and a bright summer morning. *Victory* had been back in England a mere five days after arriving from the Caribbean. Nelson, we were told by the officer of the supply crew, had gone at once to London. The ship's crew were busy making repairs and entertaining their own visitors aboard ship. 'It's not a sight for sensitive souls, Jack Tars enjoying themselves in harbour, so just prepare yourselves,' he warned.

I thought it was a great shame that these men were denied the chance of shore leave. They were imprisoned, as I had been in the past, while their officers were allowed to go ashore. I thought to say it, then decided not to. Play the game, Sam. But at that moment, I also could not help feeling a burst of glee. I was now among that number. I would be able to go ashore when the ship arrived in harbour. I had leave.

The fleet was moored at Spithead, the broad stretch of water separating Portsmouth and the Isle of Wight. As the boat bobbed towards this great line of ships, I wondered which one was *Victory*. It soon became clear. Approaching from the stern, I was astonished by her size. The mainmast stood taller than a church spire.

The great cabins at her stern rose like a grand three-storey town house, the windows decorated in intricate gold and black. In the past, when entering a Navy ship, I could only wonder what comfort lay behind those windows. Now, I could expect to visit these luxurious oases to dine occasionally with the Captain or the officers. Perhaps Lord Nelson himself would invite the midshipmen to dinner. This change in fortune made me light-headed.

Robert stared up, his admiration written all over his face. 'They say she cost more than sixty thousand pounds to build. Seeing her, I can say she's worth every penny.'

In those moments, before we disembarked, I felt so proud to be boarding this gigantic vessel, and I forgot my misgivings and fears. Country bumpkin Sam Witchall was now a serving officer in one of the Royal Navy's most famous ships.

The supply boat bumped alongside, and we clambered up the boarding steps to the entry port on the middle gun deck. Our sea chests were winched aboard. Looking around, I could see that 24 pounder cannons stretched either side from the bow down to the officers' ward-room. A midshipman of similar age to us marched briskly up and introduced himself as William Duffy. 'Good morning, gentlemen, and welcome to the *Victory*. Captain Hardy is expecting you.'

We vaulted up the companionways to the upper gun deck and then the quarterdeck. I was so busy trying to acquaint myself with the size and magnificence of the ship, I barely noticed the sailors all touching their caps as we walked by. It didn't feel right, but I would get used to it.

There was another distraction too. Most of the crew were down in the lower gun deck, where there seemed to be some kind of riot going on. The noise was not angry, just boisterous. I could make out the sound of women quarrelling and men cheering and heckling as they would at a boxing match or cockfight. The smell of stale beer and spirits drifted up with an intensity that almost masked the stink of the bilges and the usual smells of hemp and tar.

Hardy was there in his cabin at the end of the quarterdeck. Whenever I went into the Captain's cabin of a ship, I was always amazed at the amount of space he was given. Twenty men could probably sleep in these quarters. An imposing, stubborn-faced man, Hardy was easy to remember. We had met briefly before. He greeted Robert and me politely but formally.

'So what have we here?' he said, peering at an Admiralty letter. 'Neville. You've been on the *Elephant*. Did you see action in Copenhagen?'

Robert was about to speak when Hardy turned to me. 'And you, Witchall. I hear you have a most interesting history.'

'Yes, sir.' Did he want me to tell him? Did he know? An awkward silence hung in the air. I felt uncomfortable.

He peered at me. 'You look familiar. Where have I seen you before?'

'Copenhagen, sir. I was on the *Elephant* too, and at the oars of the boat you took out to the Danish line.' I didn't want to tell him he had been on the court martial that had sentenced me to death. I had hoped he wouldn't recognise me at all.

'Of course you were,' said Hardy vaguely. 'I have it on good authority you are both brave and resourceful boys. Neville, you are approaching six years' service. You will soon be eligible for the Admiralty exam. I hope to see you serving as a lieutenant before long. Witchall, you still have a great deal to learn. Tell me, can you instruct the people in the operation of the guns or small arms?'

'I've been in combat several times, sir,' I replied. 'I've been a powder boy on the guns and I've been a boarder.'

'And how are you in the sails? Can you be relied on to climb to the main topgallant royal and ensure the topmen perform their duty with spirit?'

'Yes, sir.'

'Good. What about the sea sciences? How's your navigation?'

'I can operate a sextant, sir, and I know my constellations. But I'm anxious to learn more about trigonometry.'

'That's what I expected,' said Hardy. 'Now's your chance to catch up. I've seen a few fellows from the lower deck blossom into fine officers, and I dare say you'll be no exception. Enrol with the schoolmaster. He'll teach you the science you need to navigate a ship. Work hard, Witchall. You've got a lot of catching up to do. All the midshipmen your age will know their navigation backwards.

'For the moment, I'm assigning you both to Lieutenant Pasco, the flag officer. You will serve on the poop deck and also assist any quarterdeck officers as required.'

That was it. 'Duffy will show you to your quarters.'

Robert had warned me that the midshipmen's berth down on the orlop deck would be crowded. But I had paid him no heed. I was used to crowded quarters. In the Navy a seaman had no more than fourteen inches to sling his hammock. The orlop deck might be damp, airless and without any natural light, but very few of the crew slept down there so there was bound to be space.

We passed down the companionways that led us into the belly of the ship. Pausing briefly on the lower gun deck, I took in a scene that my eyes could scarcely believe. Men were staggering almost senselessly drunk whilst others coupled shamelessly with rough women. Two hulking brutes sat either side of a sea chest and were punching each other to kingdom come while others gathered around to egg them on. The spectators' cries of anger and encouragement left us in no doubt that a lot of money was riding on the outcome of this fight. These were the men I would have to command.

The lower gun deck was just above the waterline and light enough came through open gun ports. But as we continued down we entered the forbidding world of the orlop deck. Here, below the waves but above the hold, was a maze of passageways, ill-lit dingy cabins and store rooms.

Close by were the quarters of the surgeon and his assistants. Their dark work, I soon learned, was performed on the very table where the midshipmen ate their meals. Amid the other pestilent stinks, the whiff of gunpowder tickled my nose. And the smell of mouldy bread, for the bread room was only a short way from our berth.

Our sea chests had already been delivered and stood one on top of the other by the door to our quarters. There was no one there, which surprised me. 'They must be on duty or on leave,' said Robert. 'Don't worry, it'll fill up soon enough.' Shame, I thought. I was anxious to meet my companions.

'What do you think of our poop deck posting?' asked Robert. I could hear the concern in his voice. I preferred him a little uneasy, rather than the jaunty hero he endeavoured to be.

'I think it's going to be very interesting,' I said.

He laughed. 'I'll say. But being on the poop is probably better than the quarterdeck. They say the quarterdeck always gets the worst of the enemy musket fire – that's where the ship's commanders are, after all. We're higher up there on the poop and can see across the whole of the weather deck. We're surrounded by the hammocks too, so that'll offer some protection.'

He spoke ruefully. 'Uniforms are a mixed blessing. The people fear and respect them, but they mark you out to any enemy sniper as someone worth shooting.'

I hadn't thought of that. This was the first time I had been on a ship in a uniform. Before then I had worn the usual sailor's slops. I was very proud of my midshipman's outfit. It hadn't occurred to me that it might be the death of me.

'Let's make a pact with ourselves,' I said. 'I know we've got to present a brave front to the crew and to our fellow middies and officers. But let's not pretend to be fearless with each other. I shall be as brave as I can, but I'd like to have one friend on this floating ant heap who I can talk to honestly about what I really think.'

He didn't say anything, just nodded his head. We understood each other.

'The poop deck's not a bad posting,' he said after a while. 'I know it's safer below, but when you get close enough to an enemy ship, and everyone's bludgeoning away at each other with the guns, then the gun deck can be a pretty hellish place too. And you know what the Admiral's favourite order is, don't you? "Engage the enemy more closely." That's his motto. Lord Nelson believes the only way to win a battle is to put yourself right down the enemy's throat and annihilate him. It certainly worked for him at Copenhagen, and I'm sure it'll work for him wherever we're going.'

'Are you certain we're heading for a battle?' I asked. 'You can never know for sure.'

'I'm certain of it,' said Robert. 'Nelson is determined to take on the French and Spanish and he won't stop until he succeeds. He's been halfway across the world chasing their Admiral Villeneuve. If we can bring them out to fight, I'm convinced we'll obliterate them. And once the French and Spanish fleet is destroyed, there'll be no need to fear a French invasion of England. If we hold the Channel, and can take our troops across at will, then Napoleon can never win. Should we fail, then his soldiers will be in London before the year is out.

'Who rules the world? Britain or France?' said Robert. 'We're here to decide the fate of nations.'

CHAPTER 17

Murder

Apart from Robert, and Captain Hardy, there was one other seaman aboard the *Victory* who I knew. One morning late in August, a week after we had come on board, I was supervising the stowing of the hammocks on the poop deck. A wiry, pasty-faced sailor caught my eye. It was Michael Trellis from HMS *Miranda*. He had bullied me when I first went to sea. I had last seen him taken away as a prisoner when we fell to a Spanish frigate.

I knew a little about him, not least that he was a Marine Society boy. The society had been set up for orphans or abandoned children to provide them a home of sorts in the Navy. Such boys had a reputation, even among tars, for being particularly rough. Many had been in trouble with the law and had been offered the choice of the Navy or prison.

I suppose I should have felt some glee, finding myself in a position of power over my old enemy. But instead, I felt a surge of pity. Like many of the men on this warm morning he was not wearing a shirt. I would guess he was twenty now – old enough to be full grown. But he still looked scrawny and underfed. I could see on his back criss-cross scarring that could only have come from a severe flogging. The injuries were not new, but I wondered if they still troubled him. When I caught his eye, he looked like a beaten dog. A dull resignation hung over him like a soggy cloak. All the spite and aggression he had shown as a lad had gone. I remembered he had nearly been shot for cowardice when the *Miranda* had fought *La Flora* and *Gerona*, and wondered if his flog-ging had come from a similar incident.

At first he did not recognise me, but when I caught him looking at me later that morning, I knew the mist was clearing. One of the Lieutenants addressed me as Mr Witchall in his hearing, and I saw him flinch. When I saw him later, I noticed he tried to keep away from me. Even when he came to pack his hammock, he acted as if I were going to strike him at any moment, or order a bosun's mate to do so.

I wondered how I could put him at ease. I meant to talk to him when I found him alone on deck. But that afternoon I passed him and several other young sailors and could faintly hear them going 'Ooo-ooo-ooo' and sniggering. I ignored it, finding it bizarre. Then the penny dropped. These were monkey noises. They were letting me know they knew I used to be a powder monkey. When I mentioned it to Robert, he was angry with me. 'Sam, you can't let a thing like that go. It's plain insubordination. You must stamp it out the instant it happens again, or you'll be the laughing stock of the lower deck.'

He was right, but I was determined there would be no violence. When I saw Trellis and another seaman on the fo'c'sle that evening, they began their monkey noises again. I called over a bosun's mate at once and simply told him to have the two of them clapped in irons.

I left them there for an hour, then went to talk to them. I thought long and hard how to play this and was determined to put on the best front I could muster. I sauntered up behind Trellis and his pal, who both seemed to be dozing as they sat slumped face forward on the deck. I called on the marine who was standing guard over them to release the other seaman. He was roughly awakened and sent on his way. Trellis dozed on uneasily. 'Hello Trellis,' I said in his ear, making him almost jump out of his skin. 'I see you've been in all sorts of trouble since we last met.'

Some of his old cockiness returned. 'Not half as much as you, *sir*,' he said with sarcastic courtesy. 'I heard you were nearly hanged for desertion.' With that, the marine guard stepped up and kicked him hard in the side. 'You'll speak when you're asked to speak,' he said sharply. I signalled to the marine to stand back. I looked Trellis in the eye, shook my head and smiled.

'What you heard was wrong,' I said. 'But listen carefully to this. If I have any cause to rebuke you again, then I shall have you flogged. Poorly packed hammock, tarrying in your caulking of the deck, slovenly work in the rigging, I shall be watching your every move. I see you've suffered a great deal from the cat already. It would be a shame to add to those scars. You can stay here for another two hours. Shame you had to miss your supper.'

Then I walked away. 'If that doesn't work,' I thought, 'then I shall have to take more drastic action.'

That final week in August I made it plain to every man I oversaw that I was not to be trifled with. During inspections I made a point of insisting every hammock or deck plank be scrubbed spotless. During the storing of supplies, if a man did not address me as 'sir', I would speak sharply to him. When I caught two Cornish lads sitting around chatting when I had ordered them to stow handspikes, I had them clapped in irons for the afternoon. I did not enjoy throwing my weight around, but I was determined to make my mark with these men. I was proud of the fact that no one I chastised had been punished with a blow of the fist or the whip.

I watched Robert at work, to see what I could learn. Now he had gained in confidence, and grown to his full height, he commanded his men with firmness and respect. They understood he was to be obeyed – his manner made that clear. But they also sensed he knew what he was doing and would treat them fairly.

September arrived and the ship filled with its full complement of twenty-four midshipmen. Our mess became very crowded. Most of my comrades were pleasant, but I felt drawn to few of them. They found out soon enough I was not 'one of them' when we talked at meal times.

On 13th September we heard the ship would soon sail, although Lord Nelson had yet to return from London. I was ordered to accompany a lieutenant, two marines and a small party of seamen to take on fresh water at Portsmouth docks. We set off in the *Victory*'s launch, some fourteen of us, and rowed for the shore. I was quite excited to be heading there. I hadn't expected to set foot on land again before we left. I noticed Trellis among the tars on the launch, but he would not catch my eye.

We pulled up close to the water supply on the dock-side and the men began to roll out barrels from a nearby store, then winch them on to the launch. It was late afternoon by the time our work was done and as we prepared to cast off it was obvious a place was vacant at the oars. Searching the faces of the men, I saw at once it was Trellis that was missing. The Lieutenant looked mortified. He was a young man, probably on his first commission and would be held responsible. He turned to me and said, 'Notify the authorities, Mr Witchall. He can't have gone far. I shall depend on you to bring him back.'

I climbed up to the quay again. I was surprised to see the Lieutenant casting off. I felt annoyed to have this problem passed on to me.

'How shall we get back, sir?' I called down.

'If you can't find a boat, we'll return tomorrow.'

This sense of trust and freedom I had as a midshipman was heady stuff. There was some instinct in me that wanted to run away as Trellis had. We were all facing battle and injury or death. I could walk out of this place – they would salute me at the gates rather than stop me. I dismissed the notion and went at once to the dockyard office. Two marines were despatched to accompany me to the main gates. 'He'll never get past us, sir,' said one of the soldiers.

A horse and cart covered by a black tarpaulin was being searched by the men at the gates. The horse clopped away. But as we stood at the entrance and the soldiers warned their comrades to be vigilant I saw a slight figure drop down from underneath the cart. 'Look!' I shouted. 'It's him.'

One of the marines immediately raised his musket and fired. I was horrified. There were people about. He could have hit anyone. The man on the horse and cart stopped at once and started to shout, 'Who d'you think you're bloody firing at?' I ran past the cart and left the marines to face his anger.

There was blood on the dirt road next to the cart. Trellis had been hit. It should be easy to catch him. But the light was fading and before me stretched a warren of narrow streets and alleys.

I lost track of him several times in this maze of back-streets but it was not hard to find the trail of blood he left behind. Desperation drove him on. It took me several minutes to catch up with him.

Following him down a back alley along the side of a warehouse, I drew my pistol and shouted, 'Hold still or I'll fire.'

Trellis was cornered. 'Go on then, Witchall, shoot me,' he said. 'I'd rather die now than be flogged to death.'

We stood there panting, trying to get our breath back.

'Don't think I won't fire,' I said. 'You're coming back with me. It'll be a court martial that'll decide what happens to you.'

Trellis's eyes darted around. I could see he was weighing up the odds. He was pushing me as far as he dared. 'They'll flog me round the fleet,' he said, his voice betraying his desperation. 'Kill me, go on, kill me.'

Then, seeing I wasn't going to murder him, he carried on trying to stagger away. But he was too weak to run. Blood was running down his leg, pumping out in a steady stream.

I tossed him a handkerchief to use as a tourniquet. 'Tie that round your leg. It'll stop the bleeding.'

He sat down on the pavement, looking deathly pale.

'We'll wait here until you feel strong enough to move.'

He didn't reply. I shook him roughly. 'If we're quick, we can have you seen by a surgeon.'

'Let me bleed. I don't want to go back to that.'

I ignored him and tied the handkerchief tight around the top of his leg.

The back alley caught a ray of the late summer sun and shielded us from the autumn wind coming off the harbour. What Trellis had said was true. They would flog him, almost certainly, around the fleet. Deserting on the eve of battle was one of the most serious offences a seaman could commit. He would be an example to the rest of them. Those facing such a flogging could expect three hundred to five hundred lashes. It was enough to flay the flesh and muscle from a man's backbone. I looked at Trellis's gaunt body as he lay on the ground and knew he would not survive. The burliest, toughest Jack Tars were destroyed by such brutal punishment. Even if they lived, they would be crippled for life. It was common knowledge in the Navy that many a sailor sentenced to be flogged around the fleet begged to be hanged instead.

But what could I do?

Trellis began to ramble. 'I always looked up to sailors when I was a boy. I'd see 'em in the taverns with a girl on their arms and plenty o' money in their pockets . . .' Under his breath he began to sing a little song:

I sails the seas from end to end
And leads a joyous life
In every mess I finds a friend
In every port a wife.

He gave a bitter laugh. 'Some friggin' joyous life this turned out to be.

'I can't face it. I can't face another battle.' Now tears were trickling down his face. 'When I hear a gun go off, even when we're drillin', I just want to empty my guts . . .

'You think that makes me a coward. I don't care. I'm a coward. My mate got torn to pieces and I got covered in his guts. I wish I'd been killed too . . .'

That outburst exhausted him and he passed out.

I kept expecting the marines to hare up the alley after me, but they didn't. An idea came, clear as a mountain stream. Let him go. Leave him here. When he came round, he would be alone. With the tourniquet to staunch his bleeding maybe he could find the strength to escape.

Then I saw the marines, or at least the tops of their bayonets on the other side of a wall.

I thought to call out but something stopped me. They would be here soon. They were working their way along these passageways. They would find him. He would be treated by the surgeon and then punished. Whatever happened he was going to die. I didn't want to see him flogged to death. It was too horrible a fate for someone who had only done what I wanted to do when I was a pressed man.

I looked around. Still no one could see us. He lay slumped forward and I drew my pistol and placed it on the back of his head.

Taking a deep breath I muttered, 'God forgive me,' and pulled the trigger.

The pistol shot echoed around the alleys and he slumped forward. It was a painless way to go.

The noise brought the marines running. 'Wretch tried to kill me with my own pistol when I restrained him,' I said. They accepted that explanation without question, picked him up and dragged him back to the dockyard.

'He'll be going into the drink with very little ceremony,' said one.

I found a supply boat easily enough. I had plenty of time to think about what to say when I got back to the ship. I told them Trellis had died of his wounds when the dockyard marines had fired on him.

That night the events of the day weighed heavy on my conscience. Had I done the right thing? Had he dared me to shoot him because he thought I was too soft to actually do it? Did other seamen think I was weak too, or other midshipmen even? Why did I shoot him? To prove I was tougher than he thought? No. I badly wanted to believe I remained true to myself and my own sense of what was right and wrong.

One way or another Trellis was dead. I had helped him on his way, without pain, without the torture of a lethal flogging. But I had also killed him in cold blood. That didn't make me a murderer, did it?

CHAPTER 18

Sailing into History

L ord Nelson came aboard on 14th September. The ship was transformed by his presence. Hardy was a stern captain and the crew feared him. But the men adored Nelson. You could see it in their eyes when he walked among them.

We sailed early the next day. I had been nearly a month aboard this huge warship and was now becoming familiar with it. Was there a more extraordinary machine in existence? There were close to a thousand sailors and marines on board and enough cannons and gunpowder to destroy a city. Staring up at the acres of canvas in the towering masts, I thought it quite ingenious that mankind could build something so massive and sail it from sea to sea.

Although I fretted about my ability to perform as a midshipman, I enjoyed the privileges that came with the rank. My days were luxurious compared to how I had lived as an ordinary sailor. We were woken at half past seven, and given half an hour to wash, clean our shoes and prepare our clothes. Then we had a leisurely hour for breakfast – cocoa, fresh eggs from the hens kept on the weather deck, even fresh bread while we were close to shore, what the middies called 'soft tommy'. It all seemed unreal. Yet some of my young comrades thought the food appalling.

I was astonished to see how easily the midshipmen broke rules the ordinary seamen were expected to observe on pain of death. Some would organise 'cutting out expeditions' to the Purser's stores, to steal cheese and bread, when our own stocks ran low. An ordinary seaman would be flogged for doing that. The midshipmen often stole from each other too, especially clothes. I had known seamen made to run the gauntlet for stealing trinkets from their comrades, and then throw themselves overboard in shame.

Our privileges extended to every area of the ship. While most of the crew made do with the ship's heads, in full view of anyone on the fo'c'sle, the midshipmen were provided with 'roundhouses'. These closets offered privacy and protection from the wind and waves.

The midshipmen's day was divided into three watches, with two watches off to each one we were expected on duty. The ordinary seamen were expected to work an exhausting four hours on and four hours off throughout each day.

Some of the midshipmen's perks I found uncomfortable. The middies all had a sailor who was their 'hammock man'. He would clean their hammock every week in exchange for a glass of grog on Saturday night. Some of these men would clean clothes too, in exchange for more grog. It seemed demeaning to ask them to do this, but I was told in no uncertain terms that I was not to clean my own clothes or hammock. 'It's not a job for young gentlemen. You'll be cleaning the heads next,' hissed a lieutenant when he spotted me cleaning my hammock. I found a toothless old salt named Joshua Benedict, who was grateful for his extra ration. But when Saturday night came round, I always felt like a man giving a dog a biscuit.

From nine until noon every day I had to attend the midshipmen's school. Most of my fellow pupils were much younger than me. The older middies called them 'squeakers' due to their high voices. My schoolmates were a mixed bunch. Several were still smooth-skinned

boys, one of whom sucked his thumb. The rest, the
faces ravaged by puberty, reminded me of Robe
when I had first met him five years before on t
Miranda.

They made life hell for the ship's schoolmaster, a mi
mannered fellow called Mr Furnish. They would
shot in his blankets, or loosen the stays on his hammo
so he crashed to the deck in the middle of the night
was a wonder he never broke his neck.

He was a bumbler though, and I found his lesson
badly taught I had to go through everything
Robert again afterwards. He was happy to help me
up and was determined I should master the sea scie
I often reflected on how lucky I was to have su
friend.

Being one of Furnish's pupils I spent a lot of my
with these younger boys and some began to look
as a sympathetic older brother. James Patrick, wh
been packed off straight from his Mayfair mansion
fessed that he had expected to find 'a palace with
and was distraught to discover how squalid the in
a warship actually was. When the boys comp
about their lot, I tried to be patient with them. I
want to turn into one of those intolerant old salt
been frightened of when I first went to sea.

Stephen Rider, a likeable lad of sixteen, was
to my age in the class. He had none of the sr

or high-handedness of some of the other middies. The son of a wine merchant, he told me he'd been taken on to his first ship a year ago, as a favour to his father who had agreed to cancel the Captain's account. Rider's family were not wealthy, and he had been sent to sea with a uniform he was intended to grow into. The sleeves were far too long on his jacket, and he sometimes wondered aloud when he was going to grow sufficiently to fit his clothes. He was the butt of some of the crueller midshipmen's jokes. William Duffy, who had welcomed us aboard, sneered, 'Rider, you look like you've been swallowed by a whale and thrown up again.' Rider blushed, and I cursed myself for not being able to think of a witty retort to support him.

'Duffy isn't one of Eton's finest,' Robert said to me later. 'The greatest thing he did at school was lock a wild boar in the Headmaster's study. They expelled him for it, of course, but the Navy had no qualms about taking him. On his last ship, I heard, he would make a habit of standing on a cannon and calling over the biggest, roughest-looking tar and have him stand there whilst he punched and kicked him.'

I was aghast. 'And didn't anyone do anything about it?'

'They didn't care, was what I heard. And the man knew if he complained that would be considered mutiny. Duffy's father is Lord Holland. He's one of the

richest men in Kent. That probably has something to do with it.'

Not only was Duffy a snob, he was a boaster too, regaling us with talk of all the ladies he'd ravished and the fun he had at his club. I wasn't going to tolerate his bullying. At mealtimes he began to make a habit of stealing food from James Patrick's plate. The lad was too frightened to object. I thought drastic action was called for and plunged my knife into Duffy's sleeve, pinning it to the table. 'If you want to steal food, steal it from someone your own size,' I said to him, as quietly and calmly as I could. Duffy could hear the anger in my voice and he wasn't going to be challenged without a quarrel.

He spoke sharply: 'Mark my words, Witchall, I know people who'd slit your throat for five guineas.' I stared him in the face and borrowed a line from Bel. 'And I know people who'd slit your throat for nothing. Take any more food from Patrick and it'll be your wrist that gets pinned to the table rather than your sleeve.'

After the incident, Duffy became a constant, sneering presence, and I grew to hate his languid drawl. He also had a crony in Edward Randal, a midshipman in his late twenties. Randal had passed for lieutenant when he was twenty-one, and was a perfectly able officer, but he had no patron to champion him, and had remained a midshipman. Eight years on, he had still not had a posting and was growing bitter. When he realised Robert and his family were my friends, he could hardly conceal his envy. 'That country bumpkin who still goes to school with the squeakers,' I once overheard him say, 'even he'll be a lieutenant before me.'

Duffy and Randal would imitate my Norfolk accent whenever I spoke to them and I felt a constant need to be on my guard. At night I always checked my hammock in case the ropes had been tampered with. On more than one occasion I noticed strands had been cut, so that they would snap in the night and send me crashing to the deck. I felt only mild contempt for such schoolboy pranks. I had survived much worse.

After we'd been at sea a week, Robert and I and a couple of the other new midshipmen were invited to dine with the Captain. We were all nervous as we prepared for the evening, dressing in our best clothes and blacking our boots.

It was just my luck to be seated next to Captain Hardy. Aside from his lofty position on the ship, here was a man who was a close friend to Britain's greatest hero. I tried to bring this up in conversation: 'Might I ask when you first met Lord Nelson, sir?' I said as we spooned down our soup.

Hardy ignored my question entirely. Instead he

said, 'I'm interested in you, Witchall. Not many of our midshipmen come from the lower deck. Viscount Neville has told me about you. I know you have the benefit of his patronage, but he wouldn't back you if you were no good. What makes you tick, Witchall? What is it about you that will make you a good midshipman?'

I didn't know what he wanted me to say. Was he expecting me to boast about my great perspicacity, my formidable courage, my unwavering determination? Or should I affect modesty, or patriotism?

'Damn it boy, you must know why you're training to be an officer?' He was trying to sound good natured, but the stern Captain feared by the crew was lurking just below the surface.

'To lead men, sir.' It was the best I could offer. I'd already got the job, why was he talking to me as if I were applying for it?

'But what sort of fellow are you?'

I took my courage in my hands and gave it my best shot. 'I'm a lucky fellow, sir. My father is a schoolmaster and a shopkeeper. He taught me to read and write, and from him I gained a curiosity about the world. That's what took me to sea. I was pressed but I found myself serving with people who became loyal friends.'

I expected him to have become bored, but he was

scrutinising me closely.

'And is curiosity an asset to an officer?' he said.

'I would suppose curiosity was an asset to anyone, sir.'

He didn't respond. Instead he asked another question. 'You seem like a sensitive fellow, Witchall. Someone who would consider what the other fellow was thinking. Is that a fair assessment?'

I didn't like the direction this conversation was going, but I sensed Hardy was not a man who just expected his underlings to merely agree with everything he said. I said, 'Sensitivity is often seen as one step away from weakness, sir. And many would say a Navy man-o'-war is no place for sensitivity. But I would say that knowing how others think is an essential step in knowing how to command them well.'

Conversation around the table had died. Everyone was looking at me. I felt embarrassed. Hardy sensed this too and turned to his fellow diners. 'Carry on, carry on,' he waved his hand at them impatiently.

Then he put a hand on my shoulder and spoke quietly. 'Inquisitiveness and sensitivity are fine human qualities, Witchall, but more suited to men of science than midshipmen. What the Navy requires is toughness and an unthinking faith in giving orders. They are rough men you are commanding, Witchall. You of all people must know that. They should fear, admire and believe in you as their leader. Keep your human qualities, Witchall, but build a carapace over them, otherwise you will never survive in the bear pit that is a man-o'-war.'

This was advice to take to heart. I knew he meant well.

Apart from the Captain, the officer I was most wary of was the flag officer Lieutenant Pasco. Robert and I had both been assigned battle stations with him on the poop deck. Our chief duty here involved fetching and unfurling flags from the flag locker at the very stern of the ship, and then folding and returning them to their rightful place.

Pasco was a cold fish. But what Robert told me, from gossip heard from other middies, offered an explanation. The Lieutenant, a darkly handsome man of thirty or so, had been First Lieutenant on the *Victory* – second in rank only to the Captain. His record was formidable. Sent to sea at nine years old, he had served aboard fifteen ships before arriving on the *Victory* two years previously. With Nelson during the blockade of Toulon, he had also sailed across the Atlantic in search of the Combined Fleet.

But when Nelson returned to the *Victory* in September, he had made Pasco his flag officer and promoted another Lieutenant, John Quilliam, as his First Lieutenant. Pasco was upset about this, not least because a first lieutenant could expect to be promoted to a Captain following a successful action but a flag officer would not.

His mood was not brightened by the rheumatism he suffered. I also heard he had married during a brief shore leave the previous month, when *Victory* anchored at Spithead. He must have been disappointed to have been immediately recalled to sea.

He was often haughty and distant, but this made me more determined to make him think I was worthy of my rank. Every night, before I went to sleep, I would pore over Sir Home Riggs Popham's book *Telegraphic Signals, or Marine Vocabulary*, to assist him the best I could.

It was a taxing read, although the idea behind it was brilliant. Signalling with flags from ship to ship had changed since I first went to sea. Then, a few flags had served as basic signals, such as 'Enemy in Sight' or 'Engage the Enemy'. There was no provision for anything other than the bluntest message. But with Popham's new system, a ship's captain could speak to another ship, or an admiral to his entire fleet, with whatever words he chose. The Signals Officer used ten flags, arranged in particular formation, to either make one of five hundred commonly used words, or to spell out words letter by letter if they fell outside the five hundred.

I thought it an ingenious thing, that captain could

speak clearly to captain, beyond the hailing distance of a human voice – even over several miles if telescopes were used.

Most nights, I would get Robert to test me. Popham's system was second nature to him now, and he would instantly know which combination of three flags would make, for example, the word 'Captain' or 'Advance'. Learning the vocabulary kept my mind off other worries – not least the battle that awaited us.

Given Robert's skill in signalling, I was surprised when the two of us were summoned to Captain Hardy's cabin. 'You'll stay on the poop for now, Neville,' said Hardy, 'but battle is imminent and, when called to quarters, you are to be stationed on the lower gun deck companionway to the orlop deck, where you will be required to shoot dead any seaman deserting his post. You, Witchall, will remain on the poop deck, where you will continue to act as Lieutenant Pasco's messenger and assistant.'

Robert cautiously suggested he would be far better employed on the poop with me on the companionway, but Hardy cut him off instantly, and threatened to have him whipped for insolence. 'It makes no sense,' Robert told me as we walked back to our berth. 'You're learning fast, but I know my signals like the back of my hand.'

I shook my head in agreement but said nothing. I

wondered if Hardy had sent him below decks as a favour to Robert's father. Was Hardy trying to ensure he had a better chance of surviving the battle? I was more expendable.

With a fresh wind behind us, the journey down to the southern tip of Spain took only two weeks. By the end of September, we anchored off the port of Cadiz, where the French and Spanish fleets were stationed. The weather continued to be kind to us, despite the lateness of the season, and our ships were well supplied with fresh food from our base in nearby Gibraltar. Lord Nelson took extraordinary care of his sailors, ensuring they had an onion with every meal, and plenty of lemon juice in their grog. These provisions, he knew, would keep a man vigorous and ward off the scurvy. As we bobbed up and down in the Atlantic swell, we could see the coast off Cape Trafalgar through the haze. Training my telescope on the distant shore, I thought often of how much I would like to walk that hinterland and be free of the burden of the coming battle. At night my dreams grew more vivid and terrifying, and what could happen in the days to come preyed on my mind hourly.

CHAPTER 19

'Enemy Coming Out of Port'

After three weeks in this constant state of anxiety I started to feel a new sensation – a sort of restless boredom, as we waited for something to happen. I was settling into my role, and seemed to have been accepted by the men I had to command. Rarely now did I have to admonish a man or send a fellow to be clapped in irons. Only Duffy remained a fly in my ointment, someone whose pranks and sneers made me perpetually wary.

When I came down to the midshipmen's berth one evening to find the lock levered away on my sea chest, I immediately suspected it was him. Nothing had been stolen save the pears in calvados that we had bought in Fortnum and Mason's. I was saving those for a special occasion – to celebrate our victory or survival, or a safe homecoming at least. The ship's blacksmith repaired the damage soon enough, fashioning a much stronger clasp and lock in the process, but I was still livid about it.

I didn't want to have to fight Duffy. I knew we'd both end up covered in bruises and might be disciplined. When you have to command men, it doesn't do to have to undergo the humiliation of punishment. Midshipmen were rarely flogged. Instead, they would be sent up the mast in disgrace, for hours on end. At worst, they could be denied their rank and forced to serve as an ordinary seaman. I was determined that was not going to happen to me.

Instead, I bided my time. I found Duffy squiffily drowsy at the dining table one afternoon, and was sure I could smell the aroma of calvados brandy hanging in the air. My moment had come. He was leaning back on his chair and as his head nodded down on his chest I gave that chair a nudge with my foot and he crashed down to the deck. We were even.

*   *   *

'I'm beginning to think the French and Spanish will stay in Cadiz for ever,' said Robert one morning. He was edgy too.

The very next day a frigate off to our east hoisted a signal on its main mast. It was soon after first light so I had to peer through my telescope awhile before I recognised it. When the wind blew hard, making the flags flutter straight enough to read them, a shiver ran through me. It was number 370: 'ENEMY COMING OUT OF PORT'.

I knew that from leafing through the Popham signal book in my hammock a few nights earlier. I had thought then that to see it would mean action was imminent. Now it was actually happening and our fleet was to face death or glory. My heart began to beat faster and I ran over to Pasco at once to report my observation. 'Well done, Witchall. Go and inform the Captain.'

The honour of setting the ball rolling aboard our ship fell to me. With mounting trepidation I knocked on the oak door and was ushered into the plush interior. Hardy nodded and dismissed me. Within minutes Lieutenant Pasco was handed two signals from Lord Nelson to be run up the mast. The Admiral had intended to entertain several of his captains for dinner that night. One set of signals cancelled this engagement. Alongside it we ran up flags that read, 'GENERAL CHASE. SOUTH EAST.'

Pasco had shown me a glimmer of warmth earlier, so I dared to offer him an opinion. 'I think we may find it difficult to catch the enemy fleet, sir, given the scarcity of wind to fill our sails.'

Pasco smiled. 'Do you know of Captain Troubridge, Witchall? Fine man. Lord Nelson holds him in great regard. Troubridge likes to say 'Whenever I see a man look as if he's *thinking*, I say that's mutiny.'

This confused me. 'I'm sorry, sir, if you feel I spoke out of turn.' I cursed my lack of understanding of these people. I found it difficult to fathom their prickly etiquette, and what was and wasn't permitted. I wondered if Pasco did not like me because I was, in his parlance, from the lower deck.

But Pasco smiled again. 'It was just a jest, Witchall. You and I have an interesting day ahead of us, and neither of us may live to see the end of it. So I have resolved to treat you kindly. Don't let me down, and believe me, you will need every ounce of courage in the hours ahead.'

I smiled back. 'I have been in action several times before, sir. And I stood beside Lord Nelson on the quarterdeck of the *Elephant* at the Battle of Copenhagen.'

Pasco looked astounded. 'Did you indeed?' We had talked so little Pasco knew almost nothing about me.

We had our first real conversation as the ship sped

southward. I told him of my adventures in the Baltic, omitting to mention the court martial and the transportation. He was delighted to hear again the story about Nelson putting the telescope to his blind eye so he could not see Admiral Hyde Parker's signal to retreat. 'I never believed it to be true, but if you heard it with your own ears then it must be.'

I was glad he did not ask me what happened after the battle. My sentencing for cowardice would cast doubt on my integrity, despite the fact that I had been pardoned and the charges dismissed. Robert had warned me never to mention this incident, or the transportation to New South Wales, unless it was unavoidable.

That day Pasco was charming. I supposed he wanted to take his mind off the coming action. 'The French and Spanish don't use flags for signals, y'know,' he told me. 'Just shout at each other with speaking trumpets.'

As my period on duty came to an end, he said, 'We will catch the Combined Fleet soon enough. There is very little wind, but there is a strong swell coming in from the west, and that will carry us into the jaws of battle tomorrow. Instinct tells me this will be a fiercer fight than Copenhagen. I would imagine the Admiral intends to put himself right in the thick of it.'

With those cheery words I was dismissed. As I walked back to my quarters, there was pandemonium on every gun deck. Men were tending their cannons and sharpening their cutlasses as if preparing for the inspection of their lives. Many of the cannons now had 'Victory or Death' chalked on their carriages or barrels. The men seemed in a febrile state – greatly excited at the prospect of battle.

Robert spoke his mind. I had expected to find him bullish and chipper but he seemed quite subdued. 'It's got to be done, Sam. Let's hope it's for the best.'

I had been in action with Lord Nelson, and understood he was a great leader with a genius for winning battles. To be aboard his ship during the battle would be an honour. If I survived, I would bask in the glory of it for the rest of my life.

If I survived . . . I knew in my heart this would be a battle like no other. Single-ship combat was terrifying enough. Sailing along the fixed line of Danish ships at Copenhagen and slogging it out was murderous. But here, we would be out at sea. There would be space to manoeuvre anywhere. There might be enemy ships on both sides of us, ganging up on Admiral Nelson's flagship. It would be the greatest prize of the battle. We would engage, yardarm to yardarm, and try to pulverise the living daylights out of each other.

It was said the Spanish and French sailors were not as well trained as us. My experience had shown this to be true. But no one dismissed either nation as cowards. Their sailors would be fighting as bravely as we would.

And they were in reach of a friendly shore. What concerned me in particular was being out in the open in uniform. There on the poop deck, the highest part of the ship, I would be a target for every marksman in the fighting tops of the enemy ships. As an officer, I would be expected to stand stiffly upright, not flinching or showing any fear. Would I be able to do it? I had never been in command of men during combat. I had been expected to obey orders not give them. That night I was more frightened of appearing to be frightened than I was of the battle itself.

CHAPTER 20

Prepare for Battle

Now I was one of the ship's officers I was privy to things I would never have been told as an ordinary sailor. The signals revealed we were outnumbered. Two of our men-o'-war were in Gibraltar, resupplying, and four more had recently sailed there. At the moment we were six down from our full strength of twenty-seven ships of the line. The Combined Fleet – what we called the French and Spanish ships together – had thirty-three ships of the line. Thirty-three against twenty-one. They were daunting odds and no one could say whether our missing ships would return in time for battle.

I told myself we had the best trained crews in the world. We knew that a British gun crew could fire two or three times faster than the best of the French or Spanish. And our guns had been fitted with a new flintlock mechanism. When I first went to sea, gun crews had used slow-burning matches and a trail of powder through a vent in the breech of the cannon to ignite the powder cartridge in the chamber. It was a difficult business, for it needed skill to set the cannon off at exactly the right moment as the ship rolled with the waves. There was always a few seconds' delay between applying the match to the powder in the vent and the gun discharging. It was especially hard to lay the gun well in a heavy sea.

Now all our guns, from 12 pounders through to 32 pounders and carronades, had these new flintlocks. Once the gun was loaded and primed the gun captain simply pulled a lanyard on the lock and the gun immediately went off.

We knew, from the evidence of captured enemy warships, that their gunners had no such advantage. We had always been able to fire much faster than our foes and now we could do so with greater accuracy. Such details I drew on to comfort me during that long autumn night before the battle. I did not fall asleep until well after the larboard watch had been roused at four. We midshipmen were woken soon after, and I felt full of trepidation for the day ahead. I bade Robert farewell, but he was so matter of fact it only occurred to me later that I might not set eyes on him again.

The wind had picked up during the night but it had died down by the time I came up to the poop deck. Clouds blocked the moon and obscured the creeping dawn. I felt grateful for my thick coat, and a stab of pity for the ordinary seamen in their sailor's slops.

Pasco informed me that earlier that morning the signal had been given for our fleet to form into two columns behind HMS *Victory* and Admiral Collingwood's flagship HMS *Royal Sovereign*. We were there at the head – the most powerful ship in the Royal Navy – ready to tear a hole in the enemy line.

Standing in the cold of the morning, I knew we would bear the brunt of enemy fire for the whole of our initial attack. I wished we could be third or fourth ship back, even eighth or ninth, but I wouldn't dream of saying that to Pasco. Despite the cold aggravating his rheumatism, he was in high spirits.

On the poop we constantly swept the horizon for new signals from our frigates, who were tailing the enemy, just out of range of their guns. The Combined Fleet was heading south at full sail, intent on outrunning us and escaping into the Mediterranean.

But even now, with land in the misty distance, I knew we would get to them. Soon after first light we caught a glimpse of the enemy on the eastern horizon. The wind was in our favour rather than theirs, and that heavy swell coming in from the west would carry us towards them. As we gained on our quarry, we saw them more clearly. Among them was the Spanish first rate, *Santisima Trinidad*. She was said to be the biggest man-o'-war in the world. Even from a distance she looked formidable. I hoped we would not have to engage with her, but knowing Lord Nelson and the way he fought, I feared he would head straight for her. Pasco had a word of reassurance. 'The *Santisima Trinidad*'s said to have a hundred and thirty guns, but don't worry, the crew are bound to be a complete shambles. Probably swept them out of the gutters and inns of Cadiz earlier this week. A ship like that's wasted on them, really.'

There was something reassuringly ramshackle about the Combined Fleet. They sailed in disarray, with little attempt to keep formation. Even from a distance I could see that it would be a miracle if they got through the day without a collision somewhere along the line.

At seven that morning we were given the order to hoist the signal:

BEAR UP AND STEER COURSE EAST NORTH-EAST.

Then, shortly after:
PREPARE FOR BATTLE.

It was thrilling to be the first to know the signals for the rest of the fleet – to know what Lord Nelson was thinking before anyone else.

Nelson joined us on the poop deck and scanned the eastern horizon with his telescope. I noticed how he had aged since I had first seen him four years earlier at Copenhagen. The years at sea had taken their toll, and left their mark on his weary, weather-beaten face. It was often said that a life at sea aged a man like no other occupation. I wasn't sure of this. I suspected working in a cotton mill or down a mine would shorten a man's life far more than being a sailor, but for a gentleman, certainly, it was an arduous calling.

I noticed something else about him. Although he affected his usual nonchalance in the face of danger, he had forgotten to wear his sword. Officers of any rank were never seen on deck without their swords. Clearly he was too important to have this pointed out to him.

I saw that he was wearing his every decoration, badge of honour and insignia of rank. I felt vulnerable to enemy marksmen in my midshipman's coat and hat. He was a flaming beacon on a black night to sharpshooters in the enemy tops.

'Clear for action,' he commanded, and before he returned to his cabin the marine drummer had started to beat his call to quarters. The ship was in chaos for ten minutes, as the guns were rolled out, the sails doused with water, sand scattered on the decks and the fine furniture of the officers' cabins stowed in the hold.

I mentioned Nelson's medals to Pasco, and how they made him an obvious target. He seemed mildly affronted. 'You wouldn't understand, Witchall. A lad of your low-breeding. Those who are born to command invite danger without a care. It gives the people heart and the fire to fight with courage.'

I thought perhaps he was teasing me, but I never did know with Pasco.

Captain Hardy and Mr Beatty, the ship's surgeon, came on to the poop. They were deep in conversation about Nelson's medals too. 'I'm not going to raise it with him, are you?' said Hardy.

With *Victory* ready to fight, Nelson took a tour of the ship. He walked along the fo'c'sle and the quarterdeck, stopping to speak to each of the gun crews stationed there. He had a word of encouragement for everyone, even the powder monkeys. When he reached the end of his rounds, and stood by the companionway to the poop, the whole crew erupted in a great cheer. He turned to acknowledge them and seemed to wipe away a tear from his eye. It was a telling glimpse of the real man. I wondered if, as a young midshipman, one of his captains had ever advised him to build a carapace over his feelings. He had risen to command a whole fleet yet could still be moved to tears by the affection of his men.

From the poop deck the Admiral continued to survey the enemy fleet, all the while making little observations to Hardy, and his two secretaries, Mr Scott and Dr Scott. Mr Beatty was with them too, taking the air before he began the ghastly business of treating the wounded that were sure to flood into his surgery on the orlop deck. I wondered if I would end up on the table we had dined on, having my leg or arm sawn off, with only a leather gag to bite on to divert me from the agony.

Pasco distracted me. 'Look at them, Witchall,' he said, gesturing towards the Combined Fleet. 'They're turning back to Cadiz.' This was a sight that gave heart to every British sailor. Although the horizon was covered with enemy ships, they still feared to fight us. 'No matter,' said Pasco. 'We'll catch them and give them a thrashing whichever way they're heading.'

The manoeuvre was clumsily done. 'Bloody shambles,' snorted the Lieutenant a while later. He was clearly delighted in the incompetence of his enemy. 'The whole fleet is bowed towards the centre. If a Royal Navy fleet sailed in such poor formation, the Admiral would have his Captains' guts for garters.'

Straight line or not, they still looked a formidable wall of men-o'-war to me, and soon they would be unleashing their cannon fire upon us.

Pasco continued to mock.

'Oh, and look at this. If you train your telescope on them, you'll see they have no pattern of colour. When we get close, they'll not know who's the enemy.'

Our own fleet had all been painted in 'Nelson's checkerboard' – black hull with yellow bands running along the gun decks. This would make it plain in the heat and smoke of battle who was friend or foe. Lord Nelson had even instructed his Captains to paint the steel hoops around their masts yellow not black, to ensure correct identification in close-quarter fighting. 'Most of the enemy ships have black hoops,' said Pasco, who was greatly impressed with this attention to detail.

As we drew nearer, the officers on the quarterdeck began to fret that the wind would drop entirely. Then, the Combined Fleet would be able to retreat again into Cadiz and our chance to destroy them would be lost.

Still we pressed on, the wind rattling sails and flags, the ship's band playing 'Heart of Oak' and 'Rule, Britannia'. Occasionally the wind would change and we would hear the band on the *Temeraire* behind us, mingling with our musicians to make an unholy row.

I stood there on the crowded poop deck, among the officers, marines and sailors, alone with my thoughts. Would we be raked? I had been on a ship that was raked, and having enemy shot enter the bow and traverse the whole length of the ship was terrifying. With so many ships to fight, it was also possible that we would be 'doubled' – attacked on both sides, so our gun crews would have to fire the larboard and starboard guns both at once, rather than double up on one side, which was the usual custom.

I tried to banish these thoughts but could not. When the wind carried the drums and pipes of the enemy ships towards us, I knew the battle was about to begin.

Admiral Nelson walked up to Pasco and declared, 'I shall now amuse the fleet with a signal.'

With a twinkle in his eye, he said, '"ENGLAND CONFIDES THAT EVERY MAN WILL DO HIS DUTY."' After a pause he added, 'You must be quick, for I have one more to make, which is for "CLOSE ACTION".'

I thought this a brilliant message, though hardly amusing. He was letting his loyal crews know that their country had every faith in their courage. Then Lieutenant Pasco made a daring suggestion. 'If your Lordship will permit me to substitute the word "expects" for "confides", the signal will sooner be completed, because the word "expects" is in the vocabulary and the word "confides" must be spelled.'

Nelson replied, 'That will do, Pasco, make it directly.'

I thought that a poor idea. We all knew what was

expected of us, and the ordinary sailors knew that they would be shot dead by a marine or officer if they flinched from their duty.

Pasco and I fetched the flags from the lockers by the stern rail, and within a couple of minutes they were hauled up our mizzenmast.

I was wrong about the signal. No sooner had it been raised than a huge cheer erupted from both the *Victory* and the ships surrounding us. I hoped that the sound would roll across the waves towards the French and Spanish and scare the daylights out of them.

CHAPTER 21

Into the Fire

Soon after the signal was made we heard the first shots fired against us. They reached our ears from the tail end of the Combined Fleet, where Admiral Collingwood was leading his column. We could make out plumes of water falling short of his ship the *Royal Sovereign*. 'Why do they waste their shot and powder with such profligacy?' said Pasco. 'These are not men of calibre, Witchall. We shall make an easy meal of them.'

That first enemy barrage was the cue for the British ships to unfurl their flags, and all along the line I could see bright pennants and ensigns fluttering from our sterns and mastheads. It was a magnificently defiant sight and I hoped it would unnerve the enemy.

As we grew nearer, I could see some of their ships had hung a large wooden cross from the spanker boom behind the mizzenmast. 'It's the Spanish custom,' said Pasco. 'Scoundrels think God's on their side. They'll soon find out he isn't.'

Maybe God wasn't on anyone's side? Maybe God was angry with us all?

We saw the *Royal Sovereign* break through the enemy line a mile or so to our north. Robert had told me the *Sovereign* had recently had a copper bottom fitted to her wooden hull to hinder the accumulation of marine creatures and seaweed, and this helped speed her through the water. She was a good quarter of a mile ahead of the next British ship in the line.

As Collingwood's flagship reached the enemy, we saw, then heard, his guns roar in an almighty broadside. Whichever ship he passed was being raked, and I offered up a prayer to God to spare us from such a hideous fate. Within minutes, the area around the *Royal Sovereign* was so obscured with smoke we could only see the tops of the masts.

Nelson turned to his small group of confidants and declared, 'See how that noble fellow Collingwood takes his ship into action.'

The Admiral was always quick to praise his fellows,

from officers to ships' boys. Most officers, let alone captains and admirals, were not in the habit of handing out praise.

Fire from the enemy line started to fall regularly in front of our bows. They were wasting their shot on us too. Then two of their shots landed behind us, and I felt a tingle of fear. We were in range. The hour of battle was upon us.

It seemed foolhardy to be heading in single file into the fire of so many enemy warships, all broadside on to us, every cannon on their larboard side at their disposal. Then I had a glimpse into Lord Nelson's genius. We were coming in bow and stern to the swell, which gently lifted us up and down. The Combined Fleet, on the other hand, were side on to these great waves, and rolled deeply with every motion of the sea. In such conditions, until we were almost upon them, it would be difficult for them to fire accurately and sheer good luck to land a shot on our ships.

Nelson told us to train our telescopes on the enemy fleet and find their flagship. This was the ship the *Victory* would engage. I strained to my full height to peer through my telescope towards these warships, whose cannons were now pouring out a constant barrage of flame and smoke. It was an unreal affair and I felt terribly exposed.

Shot continued to fall around us. Our good fortune

could not last. Five hunded yards from the enemy we heard a whistle then a rip above our heads, and I looked up to see a hole in the main topgallant sail. The enemy's first hit. Other sails were hit, and our stately pace, barely more than walking speed, slowed further. This was the time we were most vulnerable to enemy attack and could not fight back. Our guns, I had heard the shouted order, had been double shotted – loaded with two cannon balls. This was intended to make our first broadside more lethal, but it meant we would not open fire until we were right on top of our enemy.

With those first enemy hits, the order was given for the gun crews to lie flat on the deck. This would reduce the casualties that might be caused by raking fire. Unless that is, a cannon ball came in at exactly deck height. Then, scores of men would be mangled where they lay. 'Stand tall on the poop deck, Witchall,' said Pasco, hauling me to my feet before anyone else noticed my actions. I stammered my apologies and felt foolish. Officers, from midshipmen to admirals, were not allowed to lie on the deck.

We inched towards the enemy line. These final minutes before we were among them seemed like an eternity. We could even see the enemy fire coming towards us, especially the tumbling chain shot or bar shot. The air seemed so full of it I wondered why more was not hitting our ship.

It was that moment Captain Hardy raised his concerns to Lord Nelson about the medals on his coat. Nelson shrugged off his suggestion, as everyone knew he would. 'It's too late now to be shifting a coat,' I heard him say.

A ghastly splintering sound rent the air above our heads. Slivers of wood rained down from the mizzen topmast. Then came an awful creak and the topmast tumbled down, held precariously above our heads by the ropes that supported it.

I felt some outrage at this hit. How dare they damage our lovely ship and the rigging we had so carefully maintained. For all their brooding menace, warships were delicate, fragile things, which needed constant attention and care to keep them at their best. But they weren't as delicate as human flesh and bone. The next shot to hit our ship whistled over the fo'c'sle, through the shrouds and ratlines and hammock nets, and destroyed our wheel and the two quartermasters steering the ship. The men were both terribly maimed and their bodies were flung over the rail. All that remained was a pile of splinters and two glistening pools of blood. Even before the steersmen had gone overboard, Hardy called for forty men to be sent to the stern to operate the ropes of the tiller by hand.

I saw Hardy and Mr Scott walking on the quarterdeck, talking as if they were out on a Sunday stroll. A few seconds later a horrible tearing of the air made me look again. Scott had been sliced in two by shot, his severed trunk pumping gore all over the deck. Hardy and Nelson had been close enough to have their breeches and stockings splashed with blood. Scott, too, went over the side.

Horror piled upon horror. A squad of eight marines close to us on the poop deck were killed by a single round of double-headed shot, which swept through them. Nothing in the world could stop me being the next gory casualty. Nelson saw this ghastly spectacle and swiftly ordered the other marines on the poop to take cover. But he and the rest of us stayed in full view of the enemy.

At each atrocity I felt the bile rise in my throat and I had trouble swallowing. I struggled to keep my upright bearing. I kept telling myself I had been in action before and should be used to such sights. Pasco sensed my fear, but did not chide me. 'Hold fast, Witchall, hold fast,' was all he said.

A cannon ball ripped through the hammock netting, throwing four or five hammocks into the air before destroying one of our boats and sending showers of splinters in all directions. Hardy and Nelson were close to that one, and I noticed Hardy look down at his shoe. I wondered if he had been wounded, but Nelson said something quietly to him and the two strolled on, seemingly without a care in the world.

This was the moment Pasco produced a small paper bag. 'Care for a grape, Witchall,' he said. 'Supply ship brought them fresh from Gibraltar. They need eating before they start to go mouldy.'

The whole situation was so absurd I had to laugh. 'Thank you, sir,' I said. 'I'm sorry I can't make my own contribution to this picnic. Still, at least it hasn't started to rain on us.'

'Only splinters and shot,' said Pasco. 'Nothing too drastic.'

I never understood this upper-class habit of behaving in combat as if one were standing in a Mayfair drawing room making polite conversation. I had seen the Spanish officers on *La Flora* do it, shortly before their ship had been blown to fragments. Perhaps Pasco was trying to calm his young charge, perhaps he wanted me to report that he had died as gallantly as he had lived.

We were close enough to see the men on the decks of the enemy ships. How awfully slowly we advanced towards them, with our sails full of holes. The enemy habit of aiming most of their shot at our sails and rigging rather than our hull had not changed.

Although we could hardly hear it above the thunder of the enemy guns, the screaming of the wounded was the only noise aboard the *Victory*. The men waited in silence, still as statues, coiled and ready, for their order to fire.

Pasco's little game with the grapes had cheered me, and I was able to watch Nelson at his most resourceful. As we closed in, one of the midshipmen spotted the *Bucentaure* – which we knew was the flagship of Admiral Villeneuve, the commander of the Combined Fleet. Rather than head straight for it, Nelson ordered the *Victory* to steer forward to the front of the enemy line. Now we were broadside to broadside, passing by the *Santisima Trinidad* and presenting the whole length of our larboard side as a target for the enemy gunners. And still we did not fire. We were deluged with shot – the dull crack of muskets now adding to the cannon balls that crashed around us.

All at once, Nelson commanded us to turn sharp to larboard and the order was shouted down to the men on the tiller. We cut through the enemy line so close to the *Bucentaure* that a sailor might have climbed on to our bowsprit and dropped down on her stern. Immediately to our starboard side was another 74, which Pasco informed me was called the *Redoutable*. They were both French.

As we wedged our mighty ship between these two men-o'-war, the order to fire was finally given. It was shamefully exciting to be sailing across the stern of a great warship, and seeing the destruction of her two tiers of beautifully carved cabin windows. It was an act of vandalism which filled me with unholy glee. As we slowly passed, our three gun decks began to discharge their cannons. As the crews in the very bow of the *Victory* fired, they were joined by our fo'c'sle carronade. This stubby cannon had a maw wide enough to disgorge a 68lb ball and a keg of five hundred musket balls into the *Bucentaure* with terrifying violence. From this shot alone arose a vast cloud of dust and debris which started us coughing and settled a grey dust on the shoulders of all on the *Victory*'s weather deck.

After the first destructive blow, our ship continued to shake from topmast to keel as the gun crews fired through the dust and smoke that billowed from the *Bucentaure*'s broken stern. The poor devils inside must have been enduring the torments of hell. Perhaps it took two minutes to sail by, and in that time we destroyed Admiral Villeneuve's flagship.

I saw cannon fire flash to the starboard side of our bow and *Victory* began to shake and splinters fly. Our foremast and bowsprit withered under the fire, and yards crashed to the deck. Judging by the way the ship trembled and quivered under my feet, I guessed that most of this shot was hitting the bow. I feared for Robert down below decks.

This barrage was the worst we had sustained yet and as the *Victory* sailed on I could see the mangled remains of men thrown overboard, so many that the sea turned red as we passed.

At that moment Hardy ordered the *Victory* hard to starboard, and as we turned we fired another broadside towards the bow of the *Redoutable*. But rather than returning fire I was surprised to see the French ship closing most of its gun ports.

Hardy ordered the *Victory* turn again, ready to deliver another broadside. As we did so, we passed so close to the *Redoutable* that our studding sails fouled her top-sails. All at once we were caught in a hideous embrace.

CHAPTER 22

Shot Through

We had taken on two men-o'-war with the rest of our squadron still behind us. Now we were entangled, rigging to rigging, yard to yard, with one. And I was afraid that the ships at the front of the enemy line would turn around to attack us. We might be a huge, powerful warship, but if we were attacked by several ships at once, we would soon be reduced to wooden splinters and fragments of flesh and bone.

But most of the ships that had been ahead of the *Bucentaure* and *Redoutable* sailed on, with no intention of turning around to aid their fellows. Pasco noticed too. 'Carry on, carry on, fellows,' he said, waving them away. I heard the sound of grappling hooks being thrown up from the *Redoutable*, which, being a smaller vessel, was lower than us in the water.

'What audacity these Frogs have! Taking on the *Victory*!' Pasco was shocked at their gall. Our marines gathered on the starboard rail to fire down on the deck of the *Redoutable*. Any of their men who had had the raw courage to begin climbing the boarding ropes must have been cut down. Their assault was quickly thwarted.

A hail of fire thudded down on our deck. The attack from the *Redoutable* was coming in two directions. On her fighting tops – the platforms set halfway up the masts – were squads of marksmen hidden among the canvas and obscured by swirling smoke.

We stood at our station, Pasco and I, awaiting any signal order from Nelson or Hardy. With so little to do, other than munch grapes, there was nothing to take my mind off the hideous circumstances we were in. I had no appetite for Pasco's grapes. I was so frightened I could barely swallow. But he chided me when I refused. 'Keep your strength up, Witchall. We shan't have time for dinner today.'

'When I've been in action before,' I said to Pasco, 'I've always been very busy. Do you find it difficult, sir, just standing here as an observer?' I thought perhaps he would barely be able to hear me over the noise of the guns, but he nodded. Then, as we stood surveying the terrifying scenes before us, he shouted, 'Observe the Captain and the Admiral. Look how bravely they stand, right there in the middle of the quarterdeck, in plain sight of the enemy. They are showing magnificent courage.'

Seeing the two of them together – one tall and broad, the other short and slight – I thought what an odd couple they made. I also noted, by the still glistening blood that stained the deck, that this was the exact spot where Mr Scott had been torn in two by a cannon ball. That is fate, to be in battle and in one spot at exactly the wrong time.

If I moved twelve inches to my right in the next second, might I miss a musket ball or might I walk right into its path? If I stood still, might a cannon ball come and take the head from my shoulders? Was this the last thing I would ever think . . . ?

Terror bloomed inside me, like a fire catching in a pile of papers. I dragged my thoughts away and looked down at the Admiral and the Captain. At that very moment I saw Lord Nelson fall to his knees in a single violent motion. Hardy turned to see what had happened, just as Nelson placed a hand on the deck to support himself. The strength left his arm at once and he fell awkwardly, soiling his jacket in the gore on the deck. Hardy lifted him tenderly by the shoulder. Pasco shouted, 'Go at once to the Admiral, and make yourself useful.'

I was at his side in an instant, and heard the Admiral say, 'They have done for me at last.' His face had drained of colour, and I could see by his twisted posture that he was in great pain.

'I hope not,' said Hardy uncertainly.

'Yes, my backbone is shot through.' I knew then that the Admiral was a dead man. I felt a great stab of pity as I thought of the suffering he would go through before his spirit finally left him.

Hardy turned to a marine sergeant and two other seamen and said, 'Take his Lordship below, we must see if Mr Beatty can save him.'

Nelson shook his head. I marvelled at the courage he was showing, and the composure with which he faced his end. 'The feeling is leaving my legs, Hardy. And I feel a gush of blood in my chest.'

I looked at all his medals still glittering there, but could see no wound. But there was a small hole in the top of his shoulder. The shot must have come from one of the *Redoutable*'s fighting tops, and sliced through his body.

'Hurry,' said Hardy, and they picked him up. 'Witchall, go with them. Render any necessary assistance.' Nelson grimaced with pain as they lifted him, but he still had the presence of mind to tell us, 'Cover my face and jacket with a handkerchief. I have one in my pocket. I do not want the people to see me. It may distract them from their duty.'

So we did. Hardy produced a large cloth from Nelson's pocket and I did my best to hold it in place as we clumsily manoeuvred him down the companionways into the bowels of the *Victory*. Even at this early stage of the battle they were slippery with blood, as many a wounded man had made this journey before us. Below the weather deck I noticed how hot the gun decks were, and began to cough in the acrid smoke. Nelson's fear of being noticed by his men was unfounded. No one took so much as a second glance at us.

The cockpit of the orlop deck, where the surgeon William Beatty was performing his agonising duty, was like a scene from some lower circle of hell. One man, who was having his leg removed on the table, thrashed about like a newly caught fish. Three of Beatty's assistants struggled to hold him down. Even with the wooden bit between his clenched teeth he still made the most distressing noise. Other men, awaiting attention and laid along the strakes, were screaming or cursing horribly. One sailor, his arm already gone and dressed with tar to stop it bleeding, was singing 'Heart of Oak' at the top of his voice, to drive the pain from his mind.

Beatty was crouched close by, examining a marine whom he quickly decided was dead. Before we could call him, wounded men recognised the Admiral, and started to shout out, 'Mr Beatty. Lord Nelson is here. Mr Beatty. The Admiral is wounded.'

Beatty came at once, and had us carry Nelson away from the cockpit to a quieter, less crowded area close to our midshipmen's berth. It was so dark here, we almost dropped him, as we stumbled on debris underfoot. We laid him down against the strakes, and Beatty set about his work. Nelson was already becoming confused, and asked who he was. 'Ah, Beatty,' he said. 'You can do nothing for me. I have but a short time to live; my back is shot through.'

My task over, I left the safety of the orlop deck to return to the carnage of the poop deck. I looked over to the Admiral and knew I would not see him alive again.

Climbing the companionways up to the weather deck my legs felt like lead, as they had on that dreadful spring morning outside Copenhagen four years ago when I was brought from the belly of HMS *Elephant* to be hanged.

On the gun decks I could see we were jammed up against the hull of the *Redoutable*, and in many places the crews had not room to run out their guns. On the lower deck they fired up, through the hull, and on the upper deck, they fired down. Whatever ghastly slaughter was taking place inside the *Victory*, it would be nothing compared to the bloodshed on the *Redoutable*. Being so close to the enemy carried its own special risks. I saw men on our gun decks throwing water through the gun ports, attempting to put out fires they had started inside the hull of the enemy ship. If the *Redoutable* was set ablaze, we could catch fire too.

On all the gun decks there were cannons overturned and destroyed on their carriages. These guns were the victims of what the men called 'a slaughtering one' – an enemy shot that had come in straight through a port and wiped out an entire gun crew.

I picked my way through the bodies and over to the companionway up to the upper gun deck. Here I stood aside for another wounded man being carried down. It was Pasco. He was bleeding badly along his right side and the sleeve of his right arm was soaked in blood. 'Grapeshot,' he said. 'Peppered with the stuff.'

'Can I help?' I asked weakly. I did not want to leave him.

'Back to the poop deck, Witchall,' he said, tugging on to my sleeve. 'Hold fast. Do your duty. Good thing you weren't there. We would both have caught it.'

It was almost a relief to emerge from the companion-way into the open air, for the noise was so great by the guns that men could only communicate by making signs to each other. I could see that the poop deck and quarterdeck were almost deserted. They had become the most dangerous place on the ship.

As if to confirm my fears, there on the quarterdeck I saw the most hideous sight. One of our gunners was going about his duty when a shot caught his hand and ripped it from his wrist. Horror-struck, he held the bleeding stump up to look at it and a second later a cannon ball caught him in the chest and took his head clean from his shoulders. Two marines ran from cover, gathered what was left of him and cast him overboard.

To our larboard I could see another vessel, where blood was running from the scuppers and down the topsides. The sight of it nearly made me vomit, and I had to steady myself on the ship's rail.

By now, the things I was seeing no longer seemed real. The battle was turning into a strange nightmare. On I went, sleepwalking to my fate, whatever that would be.

CHAPTER 23

Waiting for Death

Shot thudded down from above, close to my feet. I danced clumsily out of the way, then Captain Hardy emerged from the cover by the shattered ship's wheel and pulled me beneath. 'Stay here for now, Witchall. There's no point making signals in this fug.'

It was true. We could scarcely see the *Redoutable* through the smoke of the guns, let alone one of our own ships.

We crouched for a while, and there came a steady thump and CRUMP of explosions as men in the *Redoutable*'s tops threw down grenades on our companionways, wrecking our carefully tended decks. All that work, caulking the planking and rubbing fingers to the bone with holystones, was now wasted.

The *Redoutable* stopped raining down fire. 'Have they struck?' said Hardy. 'Perhaps their men have stopped firing because there is no one left to fire at?' said a lieutenant. That was true. Only bodies remained visible on our weather deck.

Hardy shouted down to the upper gun deck, commanding our starboard batteries to cease fire. There was a strange silence on the ship, broken occasionally by the rumble of guns from our larboard crews, firing at enemy ships on their side. Had we won this particular battle? Then, through the screaming and cannon fire, we heard a piercing cry – '*A l'abordage!*'

'They're coming aboard,' said Hardy. 'Come on, Witchall, let's see what you're made of!'

We ran out from cover with a party of marines. One immediately fell to the deck, a victim of musket fire. The rest looked above, and discharged their muskets towards their comrade's assassin, but we could not see who had fired the shot.

I ran to our starboard rail and peered over, expecting to see men from the *Redoutable* swarming up the side of our ship. But before I could take a proper look a shot whistled past my ear and I ducked behind the rail. 'Never mind that,' said Hardy, 'they're coming over the mainmast.'

Towards the waist of the ship they had swung the mainsail yardarm around to act as a bridge for their boarders. Through the smoke I could see men swarming up the ratlines and out on to the yard, armed with cutlasses, boarding axes and pistols. Our marines had seen them too, and directed their musket fire on the yard. Our attackers fell in such numbers the others lost heart and turned tail. Our men kept up their fire as the enemy clambered down and some chose to plunge to the deck rather than face being felled by a musket.

Now it was safer to lean over the sides, we fired at the deck below. I pointed my pistol at an officer and saw him drop to his knees.

But another hail of grenades from the masts above drove us back into the shelter of the poop deck. How much longer could we hold off another assault? There were so few of us still alive on the upper deck of the *Victory*.

'This is how I will die,' I thought. A midshipman fighting shoulder to shoulder with Captain Hardy. I would go out in a blaze of glory and damn the enemy to hell!

'Let us hope Collingwood's column is faring better,' said Hardy, to no one in particular.

But we were not done for, not yet. Close to our starboard side we heard an almighty broadside. The *Redoutable* rocked and trembled in the water so violently there could be no doubt that she was the victim of this attack. One of the marines raised his head to look at what was happening, and was felled at once with a musket shot through the temple. That was how I would like to die, I thought. No spilled guts, no ripped off limbs. No agonising struggle with gangrene ...

The *Redoutable* shook again – jolted by another broadside. 'It must be one of ours – come up beside her. We're saved for now!' said Hardy. I moved to look, but the Captain pulled me back as a shot thudded into the woodwork close to my head. 'That one had your name on it, Witchall,' he said.

I couldn't see which ship had come to our aid, but could make out she was a first rate like us, as she towered above the *Redoutable*. I marvelled at the courage of the French sailors – two great warships had made a vice to trap her between them, and still she fought on. Minutes before, her Captain must have thought he had all but captured us – the greatest prize in the British fleet. Now, they were certain to be massacred.

A midshipman ran through a hail of fire towards us. Hardy didn't miss a trick. 'Look boys,' he said to the marines, and pointed to where we'd seen flashes from enemy muskets. The marines fired. Two, then three men fell from the rigging. The midshipman arrived, breathless. He seemed elated to still be alive. 'Lord Nelson is calling for you, sir,' he said to Hardy.

'Tell him I shall be with him presently,' replied the Captain.

'Lord Nelson is still alive, sir!' I said. 'Perhaps his injuries are not as serious as we feared?' Hardy shook his head.

He shouted orders that our crews were to load their guns triple shot and with reduced powder. We did not want our own cannon fire to penetrate the *Redoutable* and go through to damage our friends on the other side of her. Then he sprinted out on to the quarterdeck and down below.

The ferocity of the cannon fire died down. The smoke that had made it seem we were fighting in dense cloud and semi-darkness began to clear. Through the haze, to the south, I could see a squadron of French and Spanish ships heading towards us. Were these reinforcements, or merely the van, cut off from the centre early in the battle, and now heading back to aid their comrades? Why had they left it this late? And would they still make a difference? Seeing them I was sure everything was lost. All our struggles had been for nothing. Exhausted after several hours of heavy fighting, we would have to face fresh ships and start all over again.

I stood up and walked back on to the poop deck, my station in battle. Although we were still tangled up with the *Redoutable*, the barrage of grenades and musket fire from her tops had ceased. I stood awhile on the stern, watching our enemy approach. Through the mist I could see four? Five? No, seven men-o'-war bearing down on us. They would be upon us in less than half an hour.

Then I heard cheering drifting across the water. That must mean someone had surrendered! Was it us or was it them? Across the water I could see a French flag being lowered from the mast of a nearby 74. This was one victory to us, at least.

A moment later I heard something else that gladdened my heart. 'Witchall,' yelled Captain Hardy from the quarterdeck, 'come here at once.' I ran over. 'The *Redoutable* has struck. Take a party of men on board to put down that fire in the bow. I don't want us going up in flames.'

As I prepared to leave, I saw that Robert had appeared on deck. I should have felt elated to see he had survived the battle, but numbness prevailed. Now he was overseeing a party of tars who were clearing rubble from the deck. Hardy saw him too. 'Neville, go with Witchall to the *Redoutable*,' he said. 'Make sure he keeps out of mischief.'

I was still anxious about the enemy warships coming at us from the south. But the wind had dropped, and they had made little headway. Two, I saw, had collided and lagged behind the others as their crews tried to untangle rigging and spars. 'Never mind them,' I thought, 'we're *winning*!'

Before me, on the *Redoutable*, was a tangle of netting, fallen masts and canvas. I knew that she was sandwiched between another British man-o'-war, but beyond that, there was yet another warship jammed against her. A French or Spanish ship, I was sure. We were four great warships locked together – perhaps three thousand men, bludgeoning each other to death. What a hideous way to wage war. But then, what ways of waging war weren't hideous?

I called over three sailors and two marines, and we set off over the starboard side and on to the deck of the *Redoutable*. I dreaded to think what I would find on the ship, and I feared the reception I would receive from the French crew.

But when we entered from the stern quarters, we were greeted with courtesy. Men shook my hand and, I understood from their tone of voice and manner, congratulated me on our victory.

I realised then, with shame, how often I had thought so badly of the French, feared them as monsters and expected them to be brutal bullies or craven cowards. All of our enemies had fought well today – with just as much bravery as the British tars who had beaten them.

We went at once to the fo'c'sle to help extinguish the fire there, and our men from the *Victory* helped throw buckets of water over the flames. Picking my way along the length of the ship was an ordeal. There was so much blood on the decks it painted bizarre patterns as it washed to and fro in the swell. There must have been three hundred corpses on that ship. It was a hideous sight, and made me glad for once that we threw our dead over the side as soon as they were slain. To fight among all this carnage would have killed the fighting spirit in anyone. On the *Redoutable* it appeared that only those stationed below the waterline had survived.

CHAPTER 24

The *Ariane*

Below deck on the *Redoutable*, as we waded through the gore and bodies trying to sort the wounded from the dead, we felt the ship lurch in the water. Caught as we were, in the middle of four ships jammed together, that could only be the *Victory*, disentangling herself.

Sure enough, ten minutes later, while carrying one man up to the weather deck, I saw the *Victory* sailing away from us. We would have to rejoin her later. Pushing away from the *Redoutable*, she had left her to the British warship that had come to our rescue earlier at such a crucial moment. I could now see this was the *Temeraire*. Hailing across to her I also discovered the name of the fourth ship in this lethal tangle. There on *Temeraire*'s starboard side was another French 74, *Fougueux*. She too had surrendered.

I looked around for the French and Spanish squadron I had seen heading towards us. They were nowhere to be seen. Had they given up the fight and scattered?

When there was nothing more we could do aboard the *Redoutable*, we left her for the *Temeraire*. I approached a lieutenant, seeking passage back to the *Victory*.

'We don't have a boat available,' he told us, 'but you can join a prize crew for the *Fougueux* or make yourself useful over there.' He waved towards another French ship drifting close by on the starboard side.

She was a 74 by the look of her. *Ariane* was the name on her stern. She had struck and was on fire at the fo'c'sle and in obvious need of assistance. The *Temeraire* was sending a small number of her crew over to help, in a jollyboat.

This was the moment I first began to think we were winning this battle. Three French ships in our immediate vicinity had struck. Perhaps we were having similar successes up and down the line?

'Let's join the *Ariane* rather than the *Fougueux*,' said Robert discreetly. 'I want to get back to the *Victory* by the end of the day, rather than get stuck with another crew on a captured ship.'

I agreed. I would feel more confident on my own ship, rather than with strangers. The sooner we were back the better.

As we approached, I could see that the *Ariane* had suffered terribly in the battle. All her masts had been shot away, the stern was so badly raked that little remained of her cabin windows, and her larboard side had also taken a severe pummelling. Again we were welcomed with dignity by the French crew and its most senior officer, a Lieutenant Laruelle. The Captain had been killed early in the action, he told me in halting English. She was taking in water fast and half her pumps were broken. The smoke we could see billowing from the fo'c'sle was from a fire on her upper gun deck, close to the forward magazine. There were also two hundred wounded men among the crew. With so many dead strewn around the decks it was difficult to see who was wounded and who had perished.

Side by side with our French foes we fought the fires and pumped water from the flooding hold through the rest of that terrible afternoon. Several times we thought we had beaten the fire in the fo'c'sle, but it always burst into life again. The thick black smoke that rolled over the deck made us cough and gasp for air.

The *Ariane* continued to sink slowly in the water. As the light faded, her battered stern lay perilously close to the rising swell.

Dusk was falling when Robert came to me and said, 'Do you want to drown or be blown to pieces?'

We consulted the French Lieutenant. 'There's no hope of saving the ship now. We have to take as many men off as we can,' said Robert. He nodded solemnly.

'I shall stay here, with the wounded.'

We didn't waste time trying to dissuade him, but I thought him a very gallant man.

The stern was now so close to the water that the sea would flood in through the broken windows with every wave. The cries of the wounded on the lower gun deck became more urgent and troubled me terribly. As the water flooded in and the long open deck began to tilt more steeply, injured men would roll down the planks and into the icy water.

We had drifted a distance from the *Temeraire*, but HMS *Pegasus*, one of the 74s towards the end of our column, was within hailing distance. By the look of her she had suffered little in the action. Robert called for them to send their boats to assist us. Three arrived within minutes and we began to fill them with the French wounded we were still able to move. Those who screamed and wriggled in agony when we tried to pick them up would have to be left to their fate.

I was touched by how tenderly the British tars cared for their foes. We were all sailors after all. The *Pegasus*'s boats made three trips before the *Ariane* gave another fearful lurch and her stern slipped further under. Robert called from one of the boats. 'Hurry, Sam, her bow is almost out of the water.'

This was my final chance to escape. The *Pegasus* had already moved away, certain that the *Ariane* would soon blow up.

As I turned to go, I saw another poor fellow on the deck stir among the corpses. I had taken him for dead. Perhaps he had been unconscious. Now, seeing us leaving, he gathered his remaining strength and called for my assistance. He was an ordinary sailor and close to me in age. Both his legs were covered in bloody bandages.

'Come on, Sam,' shouted Robert again as the last boat bobbed close to the rail. 'Hurry or you shall surely be lost.'

It was not me lying there on the deck, wounded and left to die, as I had been in my dreams. It was one of my French adversaries. I could not leave him. In my sleep I had lived through the terror he was feeling.

I turned to the boat and shouted, 'Come and help me with this one!'

'There's no room,' shouted Robert above the din of the wounded and the roar of the fire. 'Hurry, Sam.'

I went over to the man, picked him up by the arms and hauled him over my shoulder. He screamed terribly, but he did not struggle. I staggered across the sloping deck to the waterline and bundled him aboard the boat like a sack of coal.

As we rowed away, the timbers of the *Ariane* gave a great sickening groan as she upended herself in the water, blazing bow now towering above our tiny boat. Debris fell on the flames and fed them. 'Pull hard, men,' shouted Robert, seeing the fire burn higher.

An explosion roared across the water, and fierce flames belched from the *Ariane*'s gun ports still above the surface. We felt the heat on our faces. I hunched down in the boat, shielding my wounded enemy. Not Robert though. He was standing proud at the stern of the boat. His pride and his training forbade him to flinch or take cover. 'Get down, you bloody idiot,' I shouted at him, instinctively grabbing his arm and pulling him forward. A moment later, the *Ariane* vanished in a great flash of light and splinters. As shards of wood and metal scythed through the air, one caught Robert at the top of his head.

Blood splattered over my face. Something fell on me – I felt the weight of it in my lap just as the heat of the explosion singed my hair. The bile rose in my throat. 'It's Robert's head,' I thought. A splinter has taken it clean off his shoulders.

I could barely bring myself to look. It was just his hat. An instant later he slumped forward, collapsing on me and the wounded Frenchman, who screamed again. I wondered again if Robert had been killed. There was a nasty gash on the back of his head, oozing out blood. His heart was still beating. 'Sit him up,' I said to one of the sailors beside me. I took off my jacket and ripped the sleeve from my shirt. 'Tie this around the wound.'

We rowed for HMS *Pegasus* and the prisoners were swiftly pulled on deck. Robert was unconscious but his eyes would occasionally flicker open. 'Take good care of this one,' I shouted as he was hauled aboard.

The mood aboard the *Pegasus* was jubilant. 'Fourteen or fifteen of the Combined Fleet have struck,' one of their midshipmen told me. 'The rest of them have fled! And not a single one of ours surrendered.' I had had an inkling the battle was going our way when we left for the *Redoutable*. It was marvellous to hear we had won such an extraordinary victory, but I felt relief rather than triumph. There would be no more killing and we could consider ourselves to have survived!

Robert came to later that evening but could remember nothing of the day, beyond the moment we left the *Victory* and entered the *Redoutable*. The Frenchman I had rescued offered me his hand when I went to visit him in the hold. '*Ami*,' he said, with some effort. The incident moved me greatly. The French and Spanish had fought so gallantly I would be proud to count them as my friends.

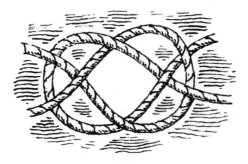

CHAPTER 25

The Storm

Robert had a brutal headache and I needed to support him when he walked, but by mid-evening he felt steady enough to risk a return to the *Victory*. Although there was little wind, the swell had picked up and we could all sense a storm was coming. We were ferried in the *Pegasus*'s smallest boat. As I boarded the boat, it lurched under me and I fell hard, banging the side of my face. By the time we reached the *Victory* I had a livid bruise from temple to jaw. I felt quite proud of this injury. I had managed to go through the entire day without a scratch. Now no one would think I had had an easy battle.

Robert was sent at once to Mr Beatty and word quickly reached me that he would remain in the sick bay for the next few days. I was glad to be back on board my own ship, but the midshipmen's mess was a melancholy place that night. We should have been euphoric, but we had lost too many men this day and seen too many hideous things. I was cheered to hear Pasco had survived his wounds, and Mr Beatty expected him to make a good recovery. Poor James Patrick had lost an arm and all that remained was a stump, though he too was expected to live. 'The poor lad,' I thought. Injuries like this on young sailors not fully grown were especially painful and slow to heal. What was left of his arm would continue to grow along with the rest of him and the stump would cause him agony for years to come.

'Where's Duffy?' I said to Stephen Rider. William Duffy's sneering presence was noticeably absent. 'Do you know where he was stationed during the battle?'

'He was down on the lower gun deck with me,' said Rider. 'He was caught by grapeshot coming in through one of the ports. Splashed his guts all over the larboard strakes. It raised quite a cheer among the gun crews.'

The mess would be a much pleasanter place without him. It was cruel to think it; all of us want to leave something worthwhile in the world, even if it's just a fond memory. Duffy died horribly, with only the cheers of men who loathed him to see his spirit away from his mangled body.

Hardy summoned all the officers to his cabin, including the midshipmen. 'The mood of the people is downcast,' he said. 'Aside from the loss of the Admiral we have nearly sixty dead and over a hundred wounded. The people are exhausted but we must keep them busy. The *Victory* is badly mauled. The hull has been much damaged by shot, especially the wales, strings and spirketing, and between wind and water. Several of the beams, knees and riders are shot through and broke, and the starboard cathead is shot away . . .'

Hardy rattled on, detailing the awful damage. My thoughts began to wander. I was in a strange, absent frame of mind.

Our men worked through the night making good the ship against the approaching storm. When they did rest, many discovered their hammocks had been shot away or drenched in blood. With every inch of spare canvas needed to mend our sails, they had to sleep on the deck. The carpenter and his crew worked throughout the night and there was no time when the ship was quiet.

There were no prisoners aboard the *Victory* but we did have one visitor from the Combined Fleet. A woman came aboard during the night, exciting much curiosity among the crew. She had been fished stark naked from the sea, having abandoned a blazing French man-o'-war. She was brought aboard the *Victory* as it was well known we had a fine selection of women's clothing for our amateur dramatic society. Lord Nelson was fond of plays and thought them a great diversion for his men.

'Sort her out, Witchall,' said a lieutenant. She was a fine-looking woman, tall with long dark hair. Someone had given her a white shirt to wear. She looked utterly bedraggled with the same kind of vacant stare I had seen on many men after a battle. I took her down to the orlop deck where the clothes were stored. She spoke a little English, and I understood that she had disguised herself as a man in order to go to sea with her husband. 'Where is he now?' I asked.

'*Il est mort*,' she said and began to cry.

Totally exhausted, I managed to snatch a little sleep but woke the next morning to the terrifying sound of wood crashing on wood. I hurried out on deck to see a main-mast yard had fallen. No wonder. A howling wind whistled in from the south-west and some of the sails set the previous day had already been torn from the yards.

The rest of that day was such a blur of frantic activity I was not able to visit Robert to see how he was. Loose sails shook themselves to tatters. Waves broke over the weather deck knocking exhausted sailors off their feet.

The ship was gaining a foot of water every hour. Men worked non-stop on the pumps to keep us afloat. As we pitched in the churning sea, stray shot rolled across the decks and the great guns slithered and strained in their moorings. 'Please God, don't let a cannon loose in this weather,' I thought. I hardly dared think of the carnage that would cause.

Peering through the rain and spray, I could see many of our ships had been forced to cut loose their prizes – either that or their tow ropes had snapped. At the farthest reaches of my vision I could see that other ships with no masts to raise sails were drifting perilously close to the shore. How terrible to survive such a bloody battle only to die in a shipwreck.

In the middle distance I saw our gallant foe of yesterday, the *Redoutable*, floundering in the water, with all her masts broken. Tiny boats from one of our warships battled through towering waves to take off her surviving crew. By the time it got dark her poop deck was almost down to the water. By the morning she had gone.

The next day and night the weather grew worse and on the morning of 24th October Admiral Collingwood, now Commander in Chief of the fleet, signalled us all to withdraw crews from the remaining prizes and disable or destroy them.

This caused much ill-feeling among the men on the *Victory*, and no doubt every other sailor in the fleet.

With so many enemy ships taken, even the humblest seaman could have expected an extra thirty pounds prize money in his pocket – two years' extra pay.

Great efforts were made to rescue the defeated sailors still aboard their ships and bring them aboard ours. We could not take part in this highly dangerous activity. The *Victory* was too damaged to help another vessel and had to be towed herself.

Robert returned to duty with a bandage still wrapped around his head. He felt unsteady on his feet and prone to sickness, but he was convinced the *Victory* would not be able to manage without him. That night we saw blazing ships in the distance, prizes set alight to stop them falling back into enemy hands, and in the morning, the carcasses of shipwrecks along the distant shore. I was grateful we had decided not to board the *Fougueux*. I heard she had been driven ashore and almost all on board had drowned.

On the evening of 28th October, a whole week after the battle, we finally limped into the safe haven of Gibraltar. Here the men were allowed on shore – usually forbidden in any port, where the fear of desertion far outweighed the boost to morale leave would provide. The worst of the wounded were transferred to the hospital.

Robert and I ventured ashore and found a small inn for supper. We were both too tired and melancholy to enjoy ourselves much and drank more than was wise, especially Robert, whose injury was still giving him blinding headaches. As we walked back, amid the wild carousing and wenching of our victorious crews, I couldn't help but feel sorry for the residents of this small port, having thousands of sailors on the rampage. It must have felt like a hurricane had hit them.

When we returned to the mess, we set about writing letters to our families, telling them we had survived the battle. A fast frigate would take our post to England much quicker than we would arrive ourselves.

Sending letters home reminded us of William Duffy. 'I suppose we ought to write to his family too,' said Robert. Certainly, no one else had offered to do so, even his friend Edward Randal. The devil got into us that evening. It was our way of letting off steam after the horror of battle. As we composed our letter, Robert and I hooted with laughter until tears ran down our faces.

Dear Mr and Mrs Duffy,

It is with great sadness I write to tell you your son died gallantly during a great battle with the French and Spanish fleets off the coast of Trafalgar.

William was a singular presence in the midshipmen's mess and we shall all miss his playful wit and wisdom.

He will be particularly mourned by the men who served
under him, whom he always treated with great kindness.

'D'you think they'll know we're being sarcastic?' said
Robert. 'I can't imagine him being any different at
home.'

That brought us to our senses. Of course his family
would know it was untrue. The letter was swiftly torn to
pieces.

I often looked at that empty place in the mess. His
trunk was still there, with his name engraved grandly
upon it. Seeing it gathering dust in the dim light of the
mess filled me with sadness. Loathsome or not, he was
just a boy. Did his family come to Portsmouth to see
him off? Him and his trunk in one of the *Victory's* boats,
rowing away from the quayside to a distant ship out in
the Solent. Did they squint through the sunshine and the
haze to gaze at the soaring masts and glinting stern galleries. I could hear them now, boasting to callers: 'You
know William is serving with Lord Nelson aboard HMS
Victory.'

CHAPTER 26

Dark Return

As we sailed north, the winter hit hard and the biting wind rarely blew in our favour. The remoteness I felt after the battle remained with me for most of the voyage. The midshipmen's mess, so often a scene of dissipation and childish pranks on the voyage out to Trafalgar, was now much quieter.

No one in England knew what had happened. Not yet. The news would take another week or so to reach them. Nelson's death, and our victory, would be relayed with equal urgency. The rest of it – reports of the thousands dead or maimed – would trickle through to anxious families in the weeks to come.

We sighted the Cornish coast at the beginning of December, and reached Portsmouth on 4th November. Back in home waters I allowed myself to feel some sense of triumph. 'We'll be heroes, y'know,' said Robert with a sly grin, 'when we go home. Right in the thick of it. It'll be sure to impress your Bel.'

At the start of the voyage I had been wary of serving alongside Admiral Nelson. But it was he who had been the victim of his audacity, along with the sixty or so killed and a hundred wounded on the *Victory*. I had been extremely lucky. On the journey back, word had gone round that we had suffered the greatest casualties among British ships during the battle. This was a source of great pride for the crew.

I wondered if we would stay at Portsmouth, or at the least send Lord Nelson's body on to London by coach. But instead we sailed on along the coast, set for the Thames, and had almost reached Dover by 12th December. Here we were engulfed in the foulest winter weather, and I feared we might be lost in the storm. 'What a cruel twist of fate that would be,' said Robert, one queasy evening as we tried to eat our supper with the ship lurching around.

It was not until 22nd December that we reached the Nore, just off the coast at Chatham. The south-westerly wind was too fierce for us to come close to the town, but we could see every flag in the harbour at half mast. This is when I realised how important our dead Admiral actually was.

Nelson's coffin was transferred to a yacht and taken up to Greenwich. That Christmas I had foolishly hoped we officers would be allowed leave, but we stayed there in the estuary. Howling wind whistled through every patched-up hole in the hull and torrential rain seeped down from the weather deck to gather in the stinking hold. We were 'awaiting orders', and they came eventually. Forty-six sailors and fourteen marines from the *Victory* were to take part in the funeral procession.

Hardy summoned me to his cabin. 'You're going, Witchall. You fought gallantly. Neville too.'

'Will you stay at Grosvenor Square?' said Robert. It was always a pleasure to visit the Nevilles' grand family home, so I agreed at once. I wanted to see Bel too. I had sent her a letter telling her I'd be in London soon. I was determined to let her know how I felt about her – maybe even ask her to marry me one day, if I became a lieutenant.

Those of us chosen to attend the funeral were taken off the *Victory* one dreary January afternoon. We sailed up the Thames in a brig and arrived in Greenwich at dusk. No sooner had we stowed our hammocks in the Naval Hospital than we were marched to a grand dining room recently built in the hospital grounds. It was here that Lord Nelson was lying in state, and it was said that fifteen thousand people had already passed through the hall to pay their respects.

We could see a large crowd clamouring to gain entry. But as soon as we arrived in the echoing marble hall – fantastic in size and ornate in decoration – the doors were closed. A great roar of disappointment rose from those outside. There would be no more visitors. We were the last.

Removing our hats, we marched slowly past the coffin. We knew it had been made of wood from the mast of a French man-o'-war. Gold motifs were painted on its black velvet exterior, the material held in place by rows of gilt nails.

The coffin looked small and I was reminded that the Admiral was quite a slight fellow. But what a great hero he was too. At that moment I felt a surge of grief for this remarkable man.

The following day we set off up river in a grand procession. Huge crowds filled the quayside to catch a glimpse of the coffin. Every boat moored there was full of people, from deck to rigging to yardarms, all desperate to glimpse a piece of history.

I started to feel quite proud of myself. Would anything I ever did be more important than fighting in the Battle of Trafalgar? Would anything I ever saw be grander than Lord Nelson's funeral? It was on such events that the world turned. We had discussed this in the mess on our way home. There would be no invasion, that was sure. There would be no further challenges to the British Navy. 'The entire Combined Fleet destroyed or humiliated, and not a single British ship surrendered,' said Robert with great pride. 'Look at the *Royal Sovereign*. She started the battle taking on ten ships at once. That kind of story'll keep any French and Spanish admiral awake at night!'

There was no doubt that the thousands who craned their necks to watch our procession thought so too. This was a tale that would be told for the rest of my life, perhaps even the rest of the century.

The next day we stood shivering in Admiralty Yard awaiting our position in the funeral procession. It was such a grand affair I doubted a king himself could be buried with greater ceremony. There were thousands of soldiers in the parade and thousands more lining the route to keep order among the crowds. When we finally set off, I noticed how quiet it was. The streets of London were packed with more people than I had seen in my life, but the only thing we heard was the beat of the bass drums in the military bands and the boom of the minute guns as we passed. Just that, and the eerie rustle of thousands of people removing their hats as the coffin went by. Some called out 'God Bless' or wept, but otherwise made no noise. It was an unsettling experience, seeing so many people making so little sound.

The funeral carriage was extraordinary – with a carving of the *Victory* figurehead at the front and a model of the *Victory*'s stern galleries at the rear. Many pronounced it magnificent but I thought it gaudy.

As we headed down the Strand towards St Paul's Cathedral, I wondered if Bel was in the crowd. I didn't see her. Perhaps she was at the back, unable to get further forward in the crush?

We reached St Paul's at about three o'clock and the coffin was placed directly under the vast dome of the Cathedral. As I stared towards the lofty gallery at its pinnacle, I thought this a fitting resting place for so great a hero.

The ceremony began with evensong. I had always enjoyed this service and as darkness fell the Cathedral was illuminated by a magnificent gas-lit chandelier. The choir sang beautifully, and when their anthems came to an end their voices hung in the air like a great silk veil, gradually falling to silence.

I thought of Psalm 107, which I knew so well from the Book of Common Prayer:

They that go down to the sea in ships, that do business in great waters; These see the works of the Lord, and his wonders in the deep . . . Then they cry unto the

Lord in their trouble, and he bringeth them out of their distresses. He maketh the storm a calm, so that the waves thereof are still.

I felt that calm and in a moment of peace I thanked God that I had survived when so many others had perished. I prayed for all of those I knew who had lost their lives at sea. I thought especially of Ben Lovett, my sea daddy on the *Miranda*, and tears welled in my eyes. He would be proud of me, I was sure of that. Then there was Michael Trellis. Had I been right to end his life? I would never be sure. And poor Lizzie Borrow, who had died in sight of home, also came to mind.

I thought too of Richard Buckley. Back on the *Victory* I would write him a long letter telling him of my good fortune. The last I heard he was sailing merchantmen from Boston all down the east coast of America and was now a third mate. 'Stay out of trouble, old friend,' I whispered fondly. I knew I would see him again one day.

The ceremony over, Robert and I were allowed two days' leave, but the ordinary seamen returned to the *Victory* immediately. Many were pressed men and fear of desertion was still upmost in the minds of their officers.

Telling Robert I would join him later at his home, I went straight to Bel's house in Bermondsey. It was nearly eight o'clock when I banged on the door. It was immediately snatched open by a lanky, dark-haired woman. It could only be her mother – she was quite a bit taller but there was enough Bel there to recognise her at once. 'You must be Sam,' she said. 'Shame you couldn't've got 'ere a bit sooner.'

'What's happened? Is Bel all right?' I blurted out without even introducing myself.

'Come in lad.' The smell of hot pie wafted towards me. 'I knew it was you. Bel don't know any other Navy midshipmen. Least not that we know of!'

I sat down in their window seat. After the cold of the evening, the house felt snug. 'She left this for you,' said her mother, and handed me a letter. Although she was thin there was nothing frail about this formidable-looking woman with hard, dark eyes. She wasn't the fire-breathing dragon of my imagination but I could see she wouldn't suffer fools. I was relieved she'd spoken to me with a smile and was making an effort to be pleasant.

'She's gone? Where?' I was shocked. 'Did she get my letter saying I was coming?'

'Settle down, Sam. It arrived the day after she left.'

I pulled open the letter, my fingers trembling, my heart in my mouth. What had happened? Had she met another lad?

Dear Sam,

By the time you read this, I shall be on a boat to India. I hoped you'd return before I went, as I wanted so much to tell you how I've missed you and also about my good fortune. Miss Lizzie's family always promised they would look out for me and they have put me in touch with a Miss Sarah Gordon who is travelling to India to be married. She has promised me a fine wage and I had to say yes – the chance to see this mysterious place was too good to miss.

I will write to you as soon as I am settled, and hope you will be able to visit me on your travels. Stay true to me, Sam, as I will stay true to you. I will come back to England, as I'm sure you will return too.

I pray you remain safe and sound.

With fond affection

Bel

xxxx

It was a shock, but not totally unexpected. 'She's been quite restless in London,' said her mother. 'Felt she was whilin' away her life workin' in that shop, waitin' for you to come back from your travels.'

I was pleased to hear Bel had missed me so much but sad not to see her. Still, she had left me a letter to treasure.

I said farewell to Mrs Sparke. 'Shame Mr Sparke's off

down the Five Bells,' she said, 'he could have met you too.'

I was relieved he was. Bel's parents, both of them at once, would have been an ordeal.

I walked along the riverside, still filled with crowds from Nelson's funeral, and on to Grosvenor Square, where Robert and his father were waiting to take me to dine at their club. The funeral had lifted a burden from my soul. It had been a beautiful ceremony and now I felt able to enjoy my freedom. The night air sparkled with frost, and stars shone cold and bright above my head, but I felt warm in my coat. I would never have thought, when I left home five years before, that the sea would give me so much. It had brought me adventure, it had brought me advancement, it had even brought me Bel. I marched on through the streets of London feeling the whole world lay at my feet.

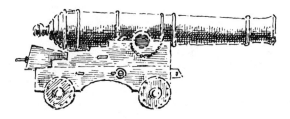

Fact and Fiction

Most of the events and characters in this book are fictitious, but when Sam arrives on the *Victory*, fact and fiction begin to mingle. Alongside Admiral Lord Nelson, his comrades Admiral Collingwood, Captain Hardy, Mr Scott, Dr Scott, Lieutenant Pasco and Mr Beatty are also real people. (All other characters, such as Duffy and Trellis, are fictitious, although Duffy often reflects the worst behaviour of some Royal Navy midshipmen.) During the battle Lieutenant Pasco did have a midshipman to assist him. Like Sam, he was also eighteen at the time of the battle and his name was John Pollard. My apologies to his descendants for writing him out of this pivotal moment in history.

The events of the Battle of Trafalgar depicted here – the details of the action, positions and names of ships – are inspired by eyewitness reports. So is *Victory*'s return to England and Nelson's funeral.

During the battle itself the *Victory* did send men aboard the *Redoutable*, and they were greeted with great courtesy by the French seamen. The incident in the book with the *Ariane* and HMS *Pegasus* is fictional, as are both these ships, although similar events occurred with British and Combined Fleet ships as the Battle of Trafalgar came to an end.

For any reader whose curiosity has been stoked by this story, here are a few of the more approachable books (from many acres) on Nelson and Trafalgar:

Trafalgar: the Men, the Battle, the Storm by Tim Clayton and Phil Craig (Hodder and Stoughton, 2004)

Fighting Sail by A.B.C. Whipple and the Editors of Time-Life Books (Seafarers series, Caxton Publishing Group, 2004)

Voices from the Battle of Trafalgar by Peter Warwick (David and Charles, 2005)

The Trafalgar Companion by Mark Adkin (Aurum Press, 2005) is a magnificently comprehensive and accessible account of both the battle and the life of Admiral Lord Nelson.

Younger readers will be fascinated by *Stephen Biesty's Cross-Sections: Man-of-War* (Dorling Kindersley, 1993), which shows HMS *Victory* in entertaining and mind-boggling detail.

Older readers will find food for thought in Adam Nicolson's *Seize the Fire – Heroism, Duty and Nelson's Battle of Trafalgar* (HarperCollins, 2006)

Finally, HMS *Victory* in Portsmouth is an unmissable treat and you can stand on the very spot where Nelson was hit. The website is brilliant too (www.hms-victory.com).

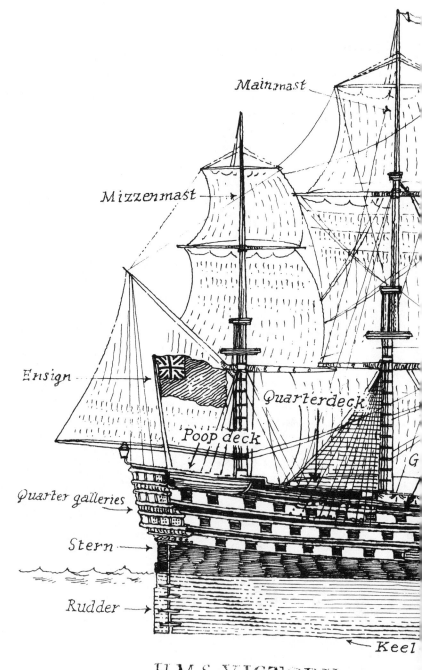

Mainmast

Mizzenmast

Ensign

Quarterdeck

Poop deck

Quarter galleries

Stern

Rudder

G

Keel

H.M.S. VICTORY

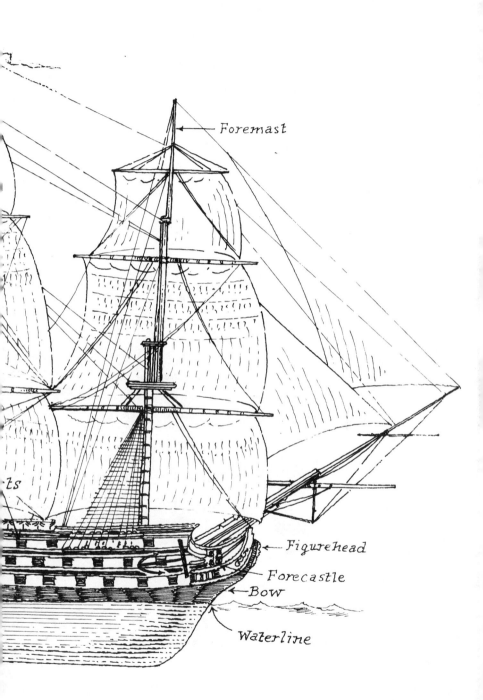

Foremast

Figurehead

Forecastle

Bow

Waterline

ts

Acknowledgements

My thanks are due, as ever, to Ele Fountain and Isabel Ford at Bloomsbury, for steering the cargo through storms and reefs, to Ian Butterworth for creating the evocative cover and Peter Bailey for drawing the fine illustrations inside the book.

While researching the book, Alison Harris at the Marine Society Library, and staff at the National Maritime Museum, Greenwich; the Department of Asia, Pacific and Africa Collections at the British Library; the School of Oriental and African Studies, University of London; the Museum in Docklands, London; the Museum of London, and Wolverhampton and Birmingham Reference Libraries all directed me to useful sources.

Thank you also to my agent Charlie Viney, for his support and encouragement, and to Mrs Julie Rose and the pupils of St Peter's Collegiate School, Wolverhampton; George Gordon, Mrs Jo Brearley and the pupils of Gresham's Preparatory School, Norfolk; Dr Roland Pietsch for his advice and for sending me his article 'Ships' Boys and Youth Culture in Eighteenth-Century Britain: The Navy Recruits of the London Marine Society'; Jeremy Lavender (for the joke), and Jenny and Josie Dowswell for their invaluable help and support.

Extra special thanks are due to Dilys Dowswell who read through my first drafts, and whose familiarity with Georgian England ensured that none of my characters used mobile phones.